"Charlie is a witness, Liz. He has seen his father's killer. We need him."

"You *need* him?" She tightened her lips before speaking again. "What about his needs? Hasn't he suffered enough without being dragged from everything he's known to live with strangers? He needs to feel safe, not scared."

Ian held her gaze. "If Charlie testifies against his father's killer, he can bring down that man—a man who could destroy many lives—more than you know."

Liz went cold, despite the lapse in the breeze that had offered relief. So that was it. They stole Charlie, hoping her nephew would give a statement that they could use in court, without caring about his emotional well-being.

"So as long as you get your killer—that's all you care about?"

Sighing, he shook his head, then looked into her eyes. "That's not true."

Books by Barbara Phinney

Love Inspired Suspense

Desperate Rescue
Keeping Her Safe
Deadly Homecoming
Fatal Secrets
Silent Protector

BARBARA PHINNEY

was born in England and raised in Canada. She has traveled throughout her life, loving to explore the various countries and cultures of the world. After she retired from the Canadian Armed Forces, Barbara turned her hand to romance writing. The thrill of adventure and the love of happy endings, coupled with a too-active imagination, have merged to help her create this and other wonderful stories. Barbara spends her days writing, building her dream home with her husband and enjoying their fast-growing children.

Barbara Phinney

Silent
Protector

Steeple
Hill®

Published by Steeple Hill Books™

STEEPLE HILL BOOKS

Steeple Hill®

Recycling programs for this product may not exist in your area.

ISBN-13: 978-0-373-67428-2

SILENT PROTECTOR

Copyright © 2010 by Barbara Phinney

www.SteepleHill.com

Printed in U.S.A.

Whosoever shall not receive the kingdom of God as a little child, he shall not enter therein.

—*Mark* 10:15

ONE

Someone was trying to run her off the road!

Liz Tate gripped the rental car's steering wheel tightly, her heart pounding in her ears as she struggled to keep the car straight.

And not careening off the edge of the newly built causeway and into the deep water to her right.

Please, Lord, help me!

The SUV beside her, some dark blue thing she didn't dare get a good look at, scraped up against her driver's side once more. A painful sound grated through her senses. The sickening shove bumped her closer to the loose gravel and rocky edge.

She swerved back, slamming on the brakes to help control her car. The tires bit into the gravel then spun and slipped farther. The other vehicle backed off.

She was losing control of the car! With a wild glance over her shoulder, she yanked the vehicle back onto the road again.

Filled with dust and gravel, her brakes squealed in protest. She fishtailed uncontrollably.

Close to the end of the causeway, the SUV beside her rammed her side again. The force knocked her against the driver's door.

Liz felt her rental spin and lurch over the gravel, catch and bump on the jagged rocks that lined the water's edge and saw nothing but slushy, dark water ahead.

She'd come down here to Florida to find her nephew Charlie, following a set of circumstances almost too fearful and incredible to believe. And now, as the hood of her rental splashed into the murky water, as that water surged over her windshield, she knew that she'd never see Charlie again.

Keep him safe, Father God. Because I've failed him again.

"Are you thirsty, son? Do you need a cold drink? Something to eat?"

But Charlie Troop sat mutely across the cluttered office from Ian MacNeal, his young eyes downcast, just as he'd been for the entire flight down here from Bangor. The child hadn't said a word to him. Not a single word. This was the boy's second full day here and still nothing. He refused to speak.

Even when the boy's hair had been shorn off yesterday, that matted, dirty mess of dark curls and knots that perpetually fell into the boy's eyes, he'd said nothing. It was too hot to bear here, Ian figured, but that wasn't the whole reason for the cut. After Charlie's hair had been trimmed down to a longish crew cut, Ian had bleached the remaining length a dark blond. He had then given the boy a pair of glasses to wear.

Charlie had studied his new look in the mirror. But after that, his gaze fell to his feet again.

It cut Ian to the core to change the boy's appearance, but his safety was too important. He needed his look altered.

Ian had tried several times to initiate a conversation with the ten-year-old, but Charlie would drop his gaze and bite his lip. And remain completely silent.

Even Ian's new assistant, Monica, a young woman whose own parents died suddenly a few years ago, tried to reach him, but Charlie stalwartly refused to speak to anyone.

Patience, Ian told himself. The psychologist who'd assessed the boy said he'd been traumatized by what he'd seen. With patience, trust and time, the child would talk. Just don't push him or he'd slip further into his mute shell, the specialist had advised.

Looking across from him this hot July day, Ian sighed. Even when he'd been a U.S. Marshal full time, long before he'd given up that life for the no-less-busy one of a pastor, he'd never had to deal with someone who so completely refused to communicate with him.

Only recalling his own turbulent youth, the gypsy lifestyle forced on him by a long line of uncaring relatives who were too busy to bother with an orphan, was he able to anticipate Charlie's basic needs. That and the wealth of experience that his neighbors, Elsie and George Wilson, could offer.

The older couple was an invaluable help. George, himself, had been a U.S. Marshal back in the day. In fact, he'd met Elsie there when she'd been hired on as part of the administrative staff. It was Elsie who had first told Ian about the need for a pastor on Spring Island, and he was happy to be working near his old friends. Especially now. Even though the Wilsons weren't officially on Charlie's protective detail, the marshals had agreed to let the boy stay in their home. Their trailer was right next to Ian's house, and they were all hoping Elsie's grandmotherly ways would have a positive effect on the frightened child.

Ian removed his cell phone pouch on his belt and dropped it on the desk, realizing only then that the phone inside was missing. For how long? He'd used it shortly after he'd brought Charlie here, but he was sure he'd put it back into the pouch when he was done.

Searching his desk caused several files to flutter to the tile floor. "It's nice and cool in here, isn't it?" he asked Charlie conversationally as he stooped to pick them up. He turned to set them on top of the filing cabinet. "Remember, I told you that this building has the only decent air conditioner in the whole village. So we'll stay in here as long as you like, okay, son? It's hotter than Bangor, isn't it?"

Again, silence. Ian looked over his shoulder at the small ten-year-old. He wanted to engage the child in conversation. Talk about the island here, about Florida and Moss Point and how the village came to be. But he knew he shouldn't name specific places. The less the child knew of his whereabouts, the safer he was. "But Elsie has a good fan. It really blows around the gulf air, and that's cool. Well, it's supposed to be cooler, I think."

Charlie made no comment.

After learning he was to be reinstated with the U.S. Marshal Service, thanks to a clause in his retirement agreement, Ian had read Charlie's case file and knew right then he had to take the child into protective custody.

Funny how he'd never expected to be reinstated after he'd retired to become a pastor. He'd seen all the legal mumbo jumbo added after 9/11, the revised nondisclosure agreements, the reinstatement clauses. But it didn't hit home until he met Charlie and was asked to return. And knew he was truly a marshal again for this very reason.

His services were needed. Charlie Troop needed a place safe enough to give his statement. The man he had seen murder his father was so dangerous that *not* convicting him could destroy any chances of a normal, safe life for the boy. Without a statement, the police wouldn't be able to prosecute Jerry's killer and hopefully bring down others high in the drug cartel for which Jerry had begun to work.

Ian stood and moved to his filing cabinet. He had a ton of other work to file away, things he'd ignored for the last month as he'd been preparing for Vacation Bible School and finishing off new programs, work he had been planning on doing before the reinstatement. The rec center here had become multifunctional, with a fully stocked clinic in back, his office up front and church in the main hall. Ian picked up a file, intent on starting some of the filing. Monica had the week off now that Vacation Bible School was over with.

But he stopped when he caught sight of Charlie. The hollow expression he cast Ian's way cut through him.

The boy was hurting—missing his father as only a boy could. Despite the fact that Jerry Troop was a known drug dealer, the man had been Charlie's father. And Charlie missed him.

"I know how you feel, son. I still miss my dad, and he died a long time ago."

Charlie blinked rapidly then bit his lips and frowned, as if fighting the urge to speak.

"Do you need to say something, son?" he gently asked the boy.

As expected, the boy didn't answer. But this time, he'd met Ian's eyes in silent but crystal clear communication. *I want to go home.*

Ian tightened his jaw against the compassion lancing through him. Being a pastor sometimes meant giving bad news but to tell the boy he had no home to go to, well, that really hurt.

Instead, all Ian could do was watch him. *Just tell me what you saw when your father died. Tell me, son, so I can stop that bad man.*

Ian had already tried that line several times on the plane coming down here but to no avail. The child was too traumatized to discuss it. He was still in shock, still trying to push aside the painful emotions until he could cope with them.

Again, Ian hated his inability to get the boy to talk. He'd been trained to deal with frightened children, and his failure here irritated him. His supervisor was expecting results, and Ian hated that he had none to offer him.

Ian searched his messy desk for his cell phone. He'd shown Charlie a picture of William Smith, the one he had on his cell. Their only suspect. But the boy had remained mute. Maybe this afternoon would be different.

Ian needed him to talk, because their only suspect wasn't the kind to allow any witnesses to live.

Abruptly, the front door banged open, the sound vibrating through the quiet building. Monica threw open his office door.

"Pastor Ian! You have to come quickly! There's been an accident. A car drove right over the causeway and into the water. Whoever's in it will drown!"

"Call 911!" Ian took flight. In one swift motion, he grabbed his hat and his handgun, as was his first reaction, then he grabbed Charlie. He wasn't about to leave the boy alone.

It was exactly as Monica had said, Ian noted as he hurried down the road, Charlie in tow. She'd said she was out for a walk and had heard the crash. A quarter mile stretch through the forest broke free at Spring Island's side of the sun-bleached, half-built causeway. It wasn't ready for public traffic, yet. But Ian could see that someone had moved the large barriers. The ferry sign still stood, though the ferry was gone. The causeway was still gravel atop larger boulders that made up the foundation.

Now in the bright sun, Ian tugged down the brim of his hat. He scanned the edges of the causeway, finding what he expected on the north side. A small car bobbed in the water. Bubbles danced all around it, and it was slowly sinking.

A woman was slumped over the steering wheel.

"Stay here, Charlie. In the shade." Ian pointed to the edge of the forest nearest the sign. Then he raced along the center of the causeway and down over the other side.

At that moment, the front end of the car dipped into the murky water, and its driver lifted her head. Ian could see water filling the interior. The woman turned to the door window, panic exploding on her face in one swift swell of fear as she slapped her palms against the glass.

"Roll down the window!" he called to her.

Ian leaped into the water, reaching the car door after one hard stroke of his arms and a push off the rocks. He caught the woman's attention. She was panicking, unable to free herself with her fevered movements.

Ian tried the door. It was locked.

"Unlock the door! Pull up on the knob!" he yelled at her.

She obeyed quickly. Working against gravity and time, Ian tugged open the door and jammed his body against it to block it from slamming shut again. The door hit his back hard as he braced himself against the frame.

Water had already lapped the woman's shoulders as the whole car sank sluggardly into the murky water between island and mainland.

"Can you undo your seat belt?"

"I don't know…it's…" Her head was barely above the water as she trailed off.

Ignoring the fear in her voice, Ian leaned over her, dipped his face into the water as he felt around for the release button. The woman gripped him in order to stay above the water line. His hat, now free, floated above him.

He found the latch and clicked it. It smacked back into his face as he lifted his head, and the car door pressed its weight against him. But the woman was free.

He pushed it open farther to allow the woman to swim out. By the time she stood on the door frame, the water had already filled the interior and was now close to their necks. The car sank deeper into the muck.

"I'm okay," she whispered breathily. "You can let go of the door now."

He did, and it splashed into the water. Finally, the whole car plunged deep down. The accident had stirred up muck and mire, obscuring any evidence of a vehicle, except for the lines of bubbles. Grabbing his hat before it floated away, Ian swam behind the woman as she dog-paddled to the rocks nearby.

She collapsed, half in and half out of the warm water, her arms splayed out and her eyes closed. Ian swam up beside her. Soaking wet curls, dark and shiny, covered her face. Ian could see her lips moving but heard nothing.

Finally, she lifted her head, with a weak lift of her hand, threw back her sopping hair. "Thank you," she sputtered out.

"Auntie Liz!"

Ian's head snapped up. Charlie was standing on the partially finished road above them, peering down at the woman with great excitement.

He'd said something!

The boy turned his attention to Ian. "That's my auntie Liz. She's come for me, just like she promised!"

TWO

"Charlie!"

With strength she didn't think she had, Liz scrambled over the rocks and up to the road. Though soaked through and still panting, she grabbed Charlie into a tight embrace.

Then, after a long moment of holding Charlie, one full of prayer and the pain of thinking how close she'd come to never seeing him again, Liz set him slightly away from her.

His front wet, he blinked up at her. "Auntie Liz! I didn't think you were ever coming! I thought you didn't love me anymore! When I called, you promised me you'd come!"

She tried in vain to contain the choke of emotion. It had been only two days since he called, but even to her, it felt like a lifetime. "Oh, Charlie! I'm here! I'm here, and I do love you very much!" Crying, she swung him up into her arms again. "I'm so sorry about your dad. It took me forever to get a flight down here. And I wasn't even sure where to go. But I found you, sweetie! I'm here to take you home now."

As she spoke, she fingered his short hair. Jerry never bothered with barbers, and the last time she'd visited, Charlie's curls had been tightening into horrible dreadlocks. But she'd held back her complaints on many an occasion, not wanting to jeopardize the tenuous hold she had on visiting the boy.

Now, his hair was barely an inch and a half in length, and dark blond, with messy streaks that mimicked the sun's effects. Gone were the gorgeous black curls of his babyhood.

She peered hard at him. And glasses? Charlie's eyesight was fine, she was sure of it. So why was he wearing glasses now?

Only then did she sense the other person on the unfinished causeway. Yes, the man who'd saved her life. She turned, slowly, feeling his presence rolling over her soaking frame.

He was tall, as wet as her, and though she knew she'd had a good look at his face as he'd rescued her, she looked at it now as if for the first time. He'd shoved back his hat, one of those soft, wide-brimmed, beige things, and because of that she got a clear view of his face.

He was handsome, but his features were tightened into a hard frown. His lips were now a thin line.

And he pointed a gun at her.

She gasped and pushed Charlie behind her, blocking the boy from the gun. She knew her bravado wouldn't last, but she ground out, anyway, "I don't know who you are or who you work for or even what your reasons are, but I can tell you that you'll be charged with kidnapping so quick it'll snap your head back! And don't think that gun is going to scare me off because it won't!"

"Who are you?"

"Liz Tate. Who are you?"

"Ian MacNeal. How do you know this boy?"

Liz felt Charlie peer around her waist. She shoved his head back. "I'm his aunt. And I'm here to take him home with me to Maine. Now, we can do this without anyone getting hurt, or we can do something stupid like you appear to be doing. It's your call."

Oh, yes, her bravado was just an act. Inside of her, Liz felt her breath stop in her throat and her fear pour ice into her heart and her whole body quiver. The wildlife refuge where she worked owned a rifle for emergencies, but no one had any need to use it. Until this minute, she'd never been close to a firearm.

Still, she refused to fail Charlie again. He didn't deserve it.

"Wait a minute." Liz straightened. "You went swimming with that gun. I doubt it will fire anymore." She tipped her head to one side and frowned.

"Besides, if you wanted to kill me, you could have *not* rescued me. So, why don't you just put that gun away and let us leave quietly?"

The man in front of her lowered his gun and shoved it into the back of his jeans' waistband. She wasn't completely sure if he had carried that gun into the water with him, but she'd let her courage speak in case he had.

"Your car is at the bottom of the inlet, and it's a long, hot walk back to Northglade. That's the nearest town." He shoved his hand onto his hips. "Are you okay?"

"Yes." She nodded, grateful to see the gun disappear behind the man's back. She still wasn't sure of the man's intentions, but logic and common sense were winning and aggravating this man would be foolish. It would be better if she stayed calm. A prayer or two wouldn't hurt, either. *Help me, Lord.* "Um, well, thank you for helping me out of there. I don't know what I would have done without you."

"You're welcome." He squinted against the sun as he scanned the shore of the mainland. His gaze returned to Liz's waist, his head tipping to one side to catch sight of Charlie. "We shouldn't stand out here. We can talk in the rec center. It's air-conditioned, and I should be able to find a few towels for us." He leaned to his left to catch Charlie's shy stare. "And you can tell me where my cell phone is, because I know you took it to call your aunt."

Liz opened her mouth to protest but shut it immediately. She peered down at the boy, whose watery, kicked-puppy look blinked back up at them. "Charlie, did you take his phone? Was that the cell phone you used to talk to me?"

"Yes. It's under my mattress," Charlie answered quietly. "But the battery's dead."

Ian lifted his eyebrows. "How long did you talk on it?"

The boy peeked up at him. "Couple of minutes," he answered in words barely above a whisper. "I just played all your games after I called Auntie Liz."

"When was that?" Ian asked.

He shrugged. "I dunno. When I first got here. I was scared."

Tears stung Liz's eyes as she fought back the urge to grab Charlie, to hold him until the fear in his voice was gone forever. She threw the man a cool look. "Don't you think you've scared the boy enough? You've stolen him from me, after all that's happened to him, and then you try to shoot me. Think about how that's affected him!" Liz shook her head quickly. "I'm surprised that he talked to you with that gun you keep waving around."

The man turned his attention back to her. "He hasn't talked at all, I'm afraid. Charlie hasn't said a word since he arrived, Ms. Tate."

He took off his hat and wrung it out. "Look, we're both soaking wet and standing in the hot sun. Why don't we walk down to the rec center? We can finish our conversation in there. The police and ambulance won't be here for another fifteen minutes at least."

"Just a minute, Mr. MacNeal—"

"*Pastor* Ian MacNeal."

Pastor? She gaped at him. No pastor she knew of would point a gun at a woman he'd just fished out of the water. In fact, no pastor she knew even owned a gun.

Seeing her hesitate, he added, "We're both wet, and if you don't mind, I don't want to be out here talking. I had told Charlie to stay put by the trees while I helped—"

He cut off his words. Liz watched him frown at the edge of the trees and then followed his gaze down to the end of the causeway, where beside a beaten sign saying Moss Point, stood a woman. She held one hand to her mouth.

The man in front of Liz cleared his throat. "Let's go to the rec center. I promise you, you'll come to no harm. If nothing else, let's go there just to get out of this sun."

True, Liz thought. The sun was brilliant today. She'd lost her sunglasses the first moment she'd been bumped by that other car. Liz stared at the murky water. Had it sunk that quickly? Was the water that deep? She quickly glanced around for the other car.

Nowhere. Maybe they *should* get off this death trap of a causeway, before whomever it was that ran her off the road came back. Which way had he gone? Onto the island, or had he turned around and sped back to the mainland? She couldn't remember. Nor was she completely sure she should tell this gun-toting pastor a thing.

With that, she grabbed Charlie's hand, putting him on the side farthest away from the man. "Lead the way."

The atypical pastor who'd rescued her led her off the causeway. Beside her, gripping her hand tightly, Charlie piped up, "Auntie Liz, isn't it hot here? Even hotter than the sun!"

"Yes, dear. Let's get inside, okay? Show me where this rec center is."

Charlie clung to her hand as they approached the young woman who stood in front of the sign at the end of the causeway. The woman clasped her hands in front of her. Tightly, Liz noticed.

"Are you all right?" the woman asked, not to anyone in particular, Liz thought.

"We're fine," Ian answered tersely.

Liz glanced up at him, surprised to see the man frowning hard at the other woman. Then she looked back at the woman. She was about Liz's age, maybe, and dressed in a cheap, plain shift dress much more suitable for the weather than Liz's dripping pants and blouse. Liz had been wearing this outfit since the day after Charlie called, the day she'd driven to the airport to catch the series of delayed flights that finally brought her down here to the southwest end of Florida.

Ian struck off ahead of Liz. For a flash, she wanted to grip Charlie's hand even tighter and charge back over the causeway again. But as Ian had said, that small town of Northglade was too far away from the forested island, and the sun was too strong. Not a good idea. Instead, Liz pulled Charlie closer and followed Ian. He was soaked, like her, and his gun stuck out of the back of his waistband.

Beside her, Charlie twisted around to peer at the woman following them along the shaded road. Liz stole her own glance, finding the woman looking curiously back at the signpost, or maybe even the water that had swallowed up Liz's rental. She didn't know and didn't care.

Around the next bend, Liz slowed her plodding walk. The closest building bore a faded sign that read Moss Point Rec Center. A small poster on the front door indicated that this past week had been Vacation Bible School. A battered bicycle had been dropped at the corner of the building. Liz stepped into the sunshine again and instantly blinked. Despite a breeze that had picked up, the humid air weighed on her like a wet cloak in a sauna.

All of what had happened lurched over her, and she stumbled over a small rock.

Quickly, Ian was there beside her, taking her free arm. "Let's get inside. There's a clinic in the back where you can lie down. I'd say shock is setting in."

It was, Liz agreed silently. Because everything was wobbling in front of her.

Ian quickly steered her inside where the cool air blasted them. The heat *was* oppressive today, the worst so far, the forecast had warned. The heat index pushed it up farther. The hot wind from the gulf lingered barely above a breeze. Ian had grown up in the northern part of Virginia where the summers got humid enough to kill. But this weather was nearly unbearable.

"Is there a doctor here?" Liz asked.

Ian shook his head as he let the front door slam behind the four of them. Cool air drenched them. "Just a nurse, who happens to be away this week attending some training seminar. You're looking at the interim nurse, and I'd say you're about to faint."

Now inside, he knew the cool air could easily get Liz Tate shivering. Quickly, with Charlie's help, he noted, Ian got Liz to the back where the clinic was. He turned when he reached the locked door and noticed Monica hurrying into his office. In the excitement, had he left his door unlocked?

A moment later, Monica raced down with the clinic's key and let them inside. Ian guided Liz to the plastic-covered exam bed at the far back, and she gratefully lay down and shut her eyes. Charlie stayed at her side.

It took Ian a moment to find where the nurse kept the towels. But when he did, he set one under Liz's wet hair and another larger one along her frame.

After lying there a moment, Liz sat up and quickly toweled herself off. For all the pale wobbliness of before, she had recovered quickly.

Then he opened the small refrigerator beside the desk and pulled out some bottles. "Orange juice. I think we could all use some. Charlie needs more fluids than the other boys around here because he's been sweating more, not that he's asked for any." He offered a bottle to her and was glad to see her take it with a quiet thank-you. "But then again, he hasn't refused any liquids, either."

She frowned at him. "Why would he ask you for anything? You kidnapped him."

He looked down at Charlie, who'd accepted his own bottle of juice. Ignoring his aunt's accusation, the boy drank deeply. *Patience,* Ian told himself. *She obviously doesn't have all the facts.*

He opened his bottle and took a long swallow. Liz had finished a third of hers before setting the bottle down on the table beside her.

"I didn't kidnap him. But before I tell you anything, I need to know one thing. How did you find Charlie? I didn't tell him where he was."

With her left arm, Liz pulled the boy close. Charlie returned the hug, setting his head down on her wet lap. "Why should I tell you anything? You say you didn't kidnap Charlie, but here he is, and when he talked to me, he sure sounded like he didn't want to be here."

Ian pulled the chair out from the desk and sat down. "Tell me how you found out he was missing."

Immediately, Liz glanced down at the boy, all the while pulling him closer.

Then she met Ian's calm stare with a direct one of her own. "I'd rather not discuss that right now."

Of course. Ian knew some of the details and guessed the boy wouldn't want to hear them all again. They did include his father's death.

He turned to his assistant. She still stood there, hands clasped in front of her. "Monica, please take Charlie down to the kitchen and make us all a snack. Liz and I need to talk."

Charlie looked up at his aunt, his expression stricken.

"He needs to stay near me," Liz stated.

"The kitchen is twenty feet away. We'll leave the door open," Ian answered. "Charlie, your aunt and I need to talk in private. It's important, okay? You know why, don't you?"

Charlie's gaze dropped, and he nodded. Again, Ian was amazed at how the boy acted. So calmly, as if he'd been simply waiting for his aunt to arrive.

"I won't leave, I promise. But—" Liz shot Ian a sharp glance "—if it's important then we need to talk. I'll be down to the kitchen in a minute, okay?"

Monica held out one hand and took Charlie away. Ian watched them leave. At the middle of the building, the rec center's kitchen was still well stocked with fruit, raw vegetables, granola bars and juice, all left over from the Vacation Bible School they'd just completed. Having a snack would ease the boy's uncertainty, he was sure.

Despite Ian's promise, the door to the clinic clicked shut behind the pair. Ian turned back to face Liz.

"Tell me how you found Charlie."

She leaned forward. "Tell me why you need to know and why it's so important."

Ian glared at Liz, only to receive an equal glare in return. "Because it is, and that's all I can say."

Liz straightened. "Then why should I tell you anything? You brought Charlie here against his will, you have someone out there acting like a sentry, ready to shove cars off the road, and then you pull a gun on me after you rescue me. So, explain to me why I should tell you anything at all. And why I shouldn't be calling the police!"

Ian leaned forward. "First up, your phone, if you had one, is sitting at the bottom of the inlet, so calling anyone will be difficult. Second, I have not authorized anyone to use force to prevent people from coming here. I would never condone that dangerous behavior. Third, Charlie was given into my custody by the police."

Liz shook her head in confusion. "Do you know what you've done to Charlie, bringing him all the way down here without someone he knows? And what right do the police have handing him over to you, some stranger? Just because you're a pastor doesn't mean you know what's best for Charlie. And while I'm at it, what kind of a pastor walks around pointing a gun at people?" She leaned forward. "So why don't *you* start talking first? Because as far as I'm concerned, I'm the one who should have custody of Charlie, not you. And be asking all the questions."

Ian folded his arms. "And where were you while Charlie's father was dragging him all over the state?"

He knew he surprised her with his knowledge of Charlie's whereabouts all these months, but with a withering look, she refused to be intimidated. "Jerry moved to Bangor a while back. I've been saving my money for a good lawyer. And part of the way through that time, I gave Jerry some of it. I knew he was going to blow it all on something stupid, but at the time, I just wanted to stay in contact with Charlie, and that was my only way. Though I realize now it was a mistake because it set me back months in my savings. The only good it did was it allowed me to see Charlie nearly every Sunday. So I took him to a church in Bangor. And out to supper."

"Okay," Ian said with a nod. "I'll answer your questions, but you have to answer a few more, first. How did you find out about Jerry's murder?"

"Like I said, I get to visit Charlie regularly. Jerry usually sleeps off a Saturday night binge, anyway. I went to their apartment last Sunday and found the police there."

"Sunday morning?"

"No, Sunday afternoon. We do something special and go to church Sunday night."

Abruptly, she pulled in a deep breath and blinked rapidly. Then she bit her lips. Both lips in a way he'd seen Charlie do when he wanted to keep quiet. "I remember telling the police who I was and…" She held her breath a bit while her chin wrinkled. "I was standing in the doorway of the apartment hoping to see Charlie." She shut her eyes. "All I could smell was…"

Ian guessed what the smell could be. He watched Liz steel herself against the memory. But obviously, her nephew was too important just to relinquish herself to her fears.

"It was awful. Jerry was a drug dealer with high hopes of making a fast million. But the police had never charged him with anything. They were investigating him. Maybe they wanted someone bigger than Jerry. Someone whose conviction would take more than just a few drugs off the street."

She lay her fingers along her eyebrows and shut her eyes tight. "But all I saw were Charlie's things splattered with blood. It was terrible." Liz bit her lips again. Then she rubbed her forehead. "I asked where Charlie was, and they told me he hadn't survived the gun battle there. I wanted to see his remains...." She swallowed a sob. "But they wouldn't let me."

Her world had crashed, he could see.

"The police said they would release the body when they were done with it. Then they drove me home." She set her head into her hands and finished off, "I went home and just cried and cried."

"When did Charlie call you?"

She looked up to show him watering eyes. "A few hours later, after I'd gone for a walk and stopped in to see my pastor. I couldn't believe it. He couldn't say where he was, but he read to me what his boarding pass said and told me he was on an island at the edge of the Everglades."

"How did he know that?"

"A friend told him about the Everglades—and the mosquitoes—and he said that some woman named Elsie said she went into Northglade for groceries. I used the satellite maps on the Internet and found this place. This had to be the place because it fit Charlie's description exactly."

Good deduction. Very good deduction, Ian thought. He hadn't considered that little Stephen Callahan, Charlie's new friend, might chatter on about where he lived. Stephen had told Ian that Charlie didn't talk to him.

Beside him, Liz groaned and lay down again. "I'm sorry," she mumbled. "I guess I got more of a scare than I thought. That guy was determined to run me off the road."

"What guy?"

"I told you. The one who came up behind me all of a sudden. It was all I could do just to keep my car on the road. He kept sideswiping me, right on the causeway."

Of course. She'd already mentioned that. "What kind of vehicle was it? Did you see the driver?"

She sighed and then sat up. "No. It was blue. A big car. I don't know what kind. An SUV, maybe? It had tinted windows, so I couldn't see inside."

Ian went cold. Liz Tate had been run off the road. And the timing of that was just too coincidental to ignore.

It could only mean one thing.

Charlie's safety had been compromised.

THREE

"Now it's your turn to talk," Liz said, coming back up to a sitting position. "When I saw Charlie two Sundays ago, he had long, dark hair. Did you cut his hair? And he never needed glasses before."

"I did. It was a rat's nest and far too hot for this weather. I also dyed it. The police offered the glasses. They don't have prescription lenses in them."

Liz absorbed what he said. "I don't understand. Sure, his hair was always a mess. I did my best, but I didn't want to get on Jerry's bad side and have him tell me I couldn't see Charlie again, so I ignored it most of the time. But glasses that aren't needed? And a dye job? Why?"

"It was necessary."

Understanding dawned on her. "You didn't want anyone to recognize him."

"I was told there was no one who would try to gain custody of him. His mother died years ago, and his father had just been murdered." He looked at her. "Is there anyone else who might claim him? Grandparents?"

She shifted on the exam table. "As far as I know, Jerry had no contact with his family. My mother lives in Portland, but she's a widow who's not well, hardly able to care for a child. Besides, she hasn't seen Charlie since my sister died. I've been trying to get custody." She shot him a questioning look. "And you simply believed what you were told about his family?"

"I had no reason to suspect that they'd lie."

"That *who* would lie? The police? They lied to me!"

"For Charlie's own safety and well within the law."

He could see that the local law enforcement officers had been prepping Liz and probably the media for Charlie's entrance into the Witness Security Program, or WITSEC. People needed to think the boy was dead.

Liz dragged in a hot breath as she sat back. "And I'm left believing he's been killed! This is not right. I'm going to take Charlie and leave. I know he'd be happy to go with me. And you don't strike me as the kind of man who'd physically stop us." She wasn't sure if that was true or not. She tossed out the threat as quickly as she shot a furtive look his way. He knew right then that she was banking on a hunch. "I won't fail Charlie like I did when his mother died. He deserves a loving environment, not getting shuffled around like a piece of secondhand furniture."

Ian bristled at her choice of words. He wasn't shuffling the boy around like furniture. He would never do that to anyone—not after living like that for years himself. "Don't be so sure. I told you that Charlie's safety is my main concern."

"Mine, too. That's why I'm here listening to you and not grabbing Charlie and walking to Northglade."

"Like I said before, I'd advise against that."

But Liz let her threat stand. "Don't tempt me," she snapped. "At least Charlie knows me and would come with me!"

From the years of being a marshal and from the few years of being a pastor, Ian knew Liz needed to vent. She didn't understand what was happening. She was only thinking of the boy's best interests. So he sat back and let her rant.

Still talking, Liz held out her hands. "How could you just take off with the boy and not consider that others might be concerned, too? The police told me nothing and scared me half to death!"

Actually, he agreed with Liz. The police had allowed her to worry herself sick, and while that was legal, they didn't tell him that she would do anything to be reunited with Charlie. And vice versa. That was a mistake.

He hated mistakes. It had been a mistake for him to be shuffled about the family after his parents died, and though it wasn't a mistake to hide Charlie down here, it was for WITSEC not to warn him about the resourceful auntie. It had also been a mistake to underestimate the nephew who could sneak away with Ian's cell phone when he was at his busiest.

Regardless, what was done was done. And at least the child wasn't as traumatized as they'd first thought. Thank the Lord for small mercies.

Would that allow Ian to focus more on the other reason he was here—to build a church? To start the social program offered by Nelson Vincenti and his wife, the couple building a resort on the north end of the island?

No. Charlie's location had been compromised. He needed to call his supervisor immediately.

But Ian couldn't ignore his parishioners for the sake of one boy, could he? Was that what God wanted him to do? Forsake his job to help Charlie? Surely another marshal could step in.

"What right do you have to take Charlie, anyway?" Liz was still blasting him. "What makes you think that you can give him what he needs when you don't even know what his needs are? What if Charlie gets sick or needs special education?"

Ian schooled his features. "His needs would be met by the Department of Justice. Or by other programs here at Moss Point. Nelson and Annette Vincenti have started a foundation here called 'The Shepherd's Smile.' It works exclusively with families in vulnerable situations providing medical care, education and Bible classes. I've been hired to implement it here. And in case you didn't notice, the children around here aren't living in the lap of luxury."

He had no plans to tell her any more than that.

If Ian was expecting Liz to show any sort of contrition, he wasn't going to get it. She shook her head, feeling her damp, dark curls bounce around. "I don't live in the lap of luxury, either. And material wealth isn't as important to me as you seem to think. But if you're here to implement a social program, then why bring Charlie here to add to the need? And for that matter, why were you approached to take him in the first place? The police gave him to you, right? It doesn't make any sense. Who exactly are you that the police trust you and not me to be his guardian? And why would the Department of Justice care about him?"

She knew at a glance that he hadn't expected her questions. Or that she wasn't about to be browbeaten. She'd lived on her own long enough to know how to stand up for herself.

"So why were you selected?" she asked, slipping off the exam table.

He sighed. He studied her before answering. "I am—I used to be a U.S. Marshal, specializing in children's safety." He noticed her deepening frown, then added, "The U.S. Marshal Service is part of the Department of Justice and handles witness security. In most cases involving juveniles, we have female officers, but some boys respond better to men than women, so a few males were also trained. I was one of them."

That made sense. Charlie had always been with his father. Relating to a man came more naturally to him.

"I left the U.S. Marshals when I accepted the call from God to be a pastor," he went on. "Then Annette Vincenti, the woman who created 'The Shepherd's Smile,' heard about me from George and Elsie Wilson and she hired me to administer her new program. It includes planting a church here in Moss Point. Until now, only a few people have been going to the Wilsons' house for Bible study. It's too far to travel to the nearest church on the mainland."

She'd heard of church planters, though the name conjured up silly pastoral images. Church planters started churches in communities that had none. They were as devoted as any missionary might be. They trained lay pastors, built churches and strengthened communities.

This was too confusing. Okay, she could see Ian in the missionary part but as a U.S. Marshal? Protecting Charlie? And yet he wasn't told about Charlie's closest relative who visited every week?

"But you retired from the U.S. Marshal Service, you said. Why are you back?"

"I also signed a little-used recall clause, something created after 9/11, I'm told. If they needed me, they could reinstate me. I could have refused because of my work here, but when I read Charlie's case file I knew I needed to help him." He lifted his chin. "And I knew I could do both jobs at the same time."

Liz walked around the clinic, stopping at the glass cabinet that held various medical supplies. "Why Charlie? He's just a little boy. He's not some snitch from the mafia."

"He's in danger."

"Of what?"

"Of being killed by the same man who killed his father."

She gasped. The man who shot Jerry would come after Charlie?

She pressed through her fear. "How? Why? I don't understand. He's just a kid."

"Charlie is a witness, Liz. He has seen his father's killer. We need him to identify Jerry's murderer."

"*You* need him?" She tightened her lips before speaking again. "What about *his* needs? Hasn't he suffered enough without being dragged from everything he's known to come down here in this heat, to live with strangers? He needs to feel safe—not scared out of his wits."

Ian had stood when she started talking but now sat down at the nurse's desk. After a thought, he pulled out his gun and began to disassemble it. He was obviously a patient man, though to try guilt on her meant he didn't know her very well. But he was patient enough to try reaching her with other tactics. "If Charlie testifies against his father's killer, he can bring down that man. But if that man stays free, he could destroy many lives—more than you know. And destroy any chance Charlie has for a normal life."

"Charlie's only ten years old! How can his testimony even be accepted in court?" She rubbed her forehead, trying to keep straight everything Ian was firing at her.

"Children younger than Charlie have testified successfully. It depends on the child, on what they saw and how it's presented in court. We're hopeful that he can help us bring his father's killer to justice."

Liz went cold, feeling the air conditioner much more. *So that was it.* They had stolen Charlie, hoping he'd give a statement they could use in court, without a smidgen of care for his emotional well-being.

No, that wasn't completely true. They needed to keep the boy safe physically first. It was reasonable to put Charlie into some kind of protective custody, and if he was emotionally secure, he'd be more likely to talk. They'd do their best to reassure him.

"Why couldn't the police in Maine just tell me that he was in protective custody?" she asked. "That he was safe? And why did they lie to you and say there was no one who would miss him?"

Ian's expression softened slightly as he took some cotton wipes from a box on the desk. "We don't tell people, relatives, friends, anything. Most of the time, it's assumed that the person in protective custody has been killed or else the person we're trying to prosecute may find the witness." He inhaled. "As for someone lying to me, that's an issue I need to deal with. And believe me, I will deal with it."

She leaned back against the wall next to the glass cabinet, feeling the cement wall press against her damp shirt. Despite the chill running through her, perspiration broke out on her skin. A cold sweat.

"It's not his safety you're worried about, is it?" she whispered, shaking her head. "He's your prime witness. As long as you can carefully guide what he says, and how he's going to say it in court, you'll get your killer." Her voice rose. "Without a smidgen of care for what's best for him!"

Sighing, he shook his head. "That's not true. His safety means more to me than his testimony."

"Really? Look around you, Ian. His father has just been killed in front of him. He's with strangers. He's lonely and scared. And who's here to look after him properly? Just you? You're busy planting a church and creating some antipoverty program. You don't have time to be a guardian or a bodyguard."

"That's why he's staying with the Wilsons. They're both retired from the U.S. Marshal Service and can help."

"More strangers!"

She turned her head away, feeling the hot sting of tears. Out the window across from where she stood, all she could see was thick forest, vines and the occasional glimpse of shimmering water through the green tangle. The beach must not be far through the trees.

Ian rubbed his jaw and then rubbed the back of his neck. He looked as disturbed as she did. "I know this is how it seems to you, but we're doing what's best for the boy. Now, we both need to shower. The water isn't safe to swim in this time of year."

She nodded. As part of her job ensuring waterfowl safety, she'd once read about certain beaches on the gulf side becoming unsafe to swim in during the month of July. Something about a bacteria.

Oh, goodie, another reason to be concerned for Charlie. She stood. "Charlie shouldn't be here."

Ian continued to wipe down the disassembled pieces of his weapon. "There's an old African proverb that says it takes a community to raise a child."

She folded her arms. "A community, not the government. And *not* here."

He straightened, turned his head and studied her. And as much as she'd like to turn away, she met his cool stare with an equal one of her own.

In that moment, she took stock of his appearance. He was really quite handsome. He had a strong faith and a caring attitude, all wrapped up inside a handsome body. His sandy hair was tousled now by the towel he'd used, adding to his trustworthy appearance. His blue eyes, flecked with white, matched the water beyond the trees perfectly.

There was more than just this feeling of security here. In his eyes, she could so easily see an inner strength, a complete and utter belief that he was doing the right thing.

Everything a Christian woman might want in a man.

No. She wasn't going down *that* path. She'd already seen what he was really like. Pastor or not, he was also a federal agent, and his only reason for wanting Charlie here was to extract a statement from him. This whole scenario was far too much of a strain on Charlie's emotional health. The poor boy had just suffered a terrible loss. She wouldn't gamble with his emotions because she had some misguided attraction to this man.

He shot her a serious look before testing and assembling his gun, the kind of look the strong, silent type offered.

But, oh, to have even an ounce of such confidence, such inner strength. Charlie would benefit so much from that in her.

"We need to learn to release our children so they can learn from others," he finally said, all the while working on his gun. "And we need to step up to bat to do our part when others release their children."

She struggled to snap out of her admiration. "Yes, I agree. Ask not what your country can do for you.

I get it. But this is not Charlie's community. Here, he's just a lonely little boy who needs his loved ones."

"He needs a community. Especially if the people who are raising him aren't where others are. Spiritually speaking, that is."

She dropped her arms to her sides and stiffened. What did he just say? Well, enough was enough. She'd accept the fact that Ian was once a U.S. Marshal who'd taken on this one last assignment. And she'd accept the fact he'd come here to start a church and implement a new antipoverty program and that he obviously felt he could do both, all with admirable confidence.

But she wouldn't accept a man she'd just met telling her that she was spiritually immature and needed to release her nephew to others so that he could grow in faith. That was stepping over the line.

"I've heard enough," she announced. "You haven't convinced me that Charlie is better off here. All you want is his statement and to train him to present it in such a way that you'll get your killer. Well, nowadays there's enough forensic science to convict the killer, and that's usually more convincing than anything else is. Let the police use that to find whoever killed his father, not Charlie."

"I'm only thinking of his safety."

"No, you're not. If you were, you wouldn't be quoting pat sayings and psychobabble. I'm thinking of his emotional health because that's just as important as his safety." She gave a frustrated sigh. "And you say you want him physically safe? Do you know anything about him? His health? What if he needs a particular medication? Has he ever had any vaccinations? What about his schooling? I'm sure you've guessed by now that Jerry wasn't big on public schooling. And has Charlie even been wearing a hat in the sun?"

She'd fired off the barrage of questions without taking a breath. Finally, drawing in air, she noticed Ian's passive expression and wondered if it was just a trained act against people who confronted him. "All you want is an airtight case against a killer who may have a good lawyer."

He wet his lips, and she found herself watching the action closely. *Good grief, why was she so physically aware of him?*

"First up," he finally said, "you're right, I don't know about his health."

He lowered his eyes, deep in thought. His mouth twisted ever so slightly as he worked his jaw. Again, she felt the tug of his good looks. *Forget that.* For all she knew, this was part and parcel of some well-schooled passiveness he'd taught himself. A subtle charm saved only for women—to get what he wanted.

"Secondly," he continued, "he owns a hat but has lost it three times in two days. Each time, Elsie or I have gone in search of it. But this time we're making Charlie look for it. Elsie thinks he's hiding it."

She shook her head and cut in, "Regardless, you've brought him to one of the hottest parts of the country and he's not used to the heat. You know nothing about him or his health! Is that wise? Or good for him?"

"While you'd take him back up north now, right back into the very heart of the danger. You don't know what kind of people you're dealing with. Nor do you realize that your coming here may have compromised Charlie's safety."

"I knew my brother-in-law a lot longer than any of the police. I knew what he was in to and how he manipulated people. He was planning to extort money from me using Charlie, and I knew he was selling drugs and would love to make a quick million dollars. I can keep Charlie safe from people like him. Besides, I found Charlie using simple logic. What's stopping others from doing the same?"

"Only if they talked to Charlie. Or followed you. It's that I'm afraid of. Thankfully, Charlie only used the phone once." Ian then pursed his lips, stopping his words as though something else had occurred to him. With a heavy sigh, he stood and pushed the chair into the desk.

Behind him, the door to the clinic opened slowly. Hearing it, Ian shoved Liz behind him. His hand reached behind his back to free up his weapon.

He had his gun out before Charlie could completely enter into the room. The boy's eyes went wide and he scurried behind Monica, who was coming in right behind him carrying a tray of snacks. She jumped when she saw the gun, and the glasses rattled together.

Immediately, Ian slipped the weapon out of sight.

Stricken, Charlie raced over to Liz. As well intentioned as Ian MacNeal wanted to seem, and as incredibly engaging as he might appear, with his position of pastor and his outward care for Charlie, there was no way, Liz decided, that she was going to get herself mixed up with him. He was exactly what Charlie *didn't* need in his life—another man with a gun. Charlie didn't need the extra stress.

And nor did she need a man who could so easily move from compassionate Christian to cold-blooded bodyguard in a blink of an eye.

Her sister had been fooled by Jerry, who'd gone from charmer to drug dealer that quickly. Those kind of chameleon men only hurt women like her who trusted people.

The sooner she and Charlie left the island, the better. Except getting past Ian, the man with a gun, wasn't going to be easy.

FOUR

Ten minutes later, after he called his supervisor and detailed what had happened, Ian called the local police to say an ambulance wasn't needed. Liz listened as he stated briefly that she'd been sideswiped by a car that roared up out of nowhere, just at the start of the causeway. Nothing more, she noted, saying as little as possible.

Within an hour, the police arrived, and together with the two officers, they returned to the causeway to stare into the murky water of the blocked-off strait.

"Why were you coming over this causeway, when you said you noticed that it was under construction?" the bigger officer asked Liz.

"The concrete blocks were at the side. There was only one sign that said Construction Ahead. It didn't say that the road was closed."

"The causeway is supposed to be closed to all traffic. I don't know why the blocks were moved."

"There's a resort being built here," she pointed out. "How did they get their equipment there?"

"Special permission. The causeway will hold vehicular weight, but it's just not finished yet, hence the fact it's closed." The highway patrol officer peeled off his sunglasses and his broad-brimmed hat and stared out at the still, dark water. He shook his head. "It's going to take some doing getting that car out of there. No one likes to get in with the snakes."

Snakes? Liz grimaced. "Should I call a tow truck or will you?"

"I can, ma'am. I know which company to call. But I don't know when he'll be able to get out here."

The other officer walked toward the island for a few feet and then turned around again. "Did you see where the car went?"

Liz shook her head. "I don't know. The engine revved a bit. I remember that, but that's all."

The officer inspected the ground. "It looks like it turned around here a few times." He looked at Ian. "Any new cars on the island that you know of?"

"No." Ian indicated the direction of the resort. "You may want to check with the resort, though. They have several vehicles. The smaller ones are vans bringing in workers."

The officer nodded. After the police took her statement and promised to call with a time when the tow truck would arrive, they left. Despite the anticlimactic way they arrived and left, Liz found herself feeling much better. She needed a shower. With the heat around her, her clothes had dried quickly, but the salt left on her skin was making her itch. She needed to clean up.

And change into what, she thought. The few clothes she'd taken were at the bottom of that inlet.

Lord, you know I need clothes. And some relief from this heat, please.

As they returned to Moss Point, she glanced around the small village. Huge, spreading trees that couldn't decide which way to grow shaded much of the hard-packed dirt street, but it was the thick, pale droops of Spanish moss hanging nearly to the ground that must have generated the village's name. There seemed to be few lawns for children, just dirt that carried in from the road until it reached the houses. In places that caught the sunlight, a few gardens had been worked. But in the heat of the summer, the vegetables looked burdened and sad.

Around them, small bungalows and trailers seemed plunked down willy-nilly. Most were simple, unadorned except by obvious poverty. Liz lived in a modest area of the country herself, and as a Christian, she tried not to focus on earthly wealth. But the brand of poverty here caught in her throat.

Several of the villagers were sitting in the shade of their homes, wisely keeping their activities to a minimum during the oppressive afternoon heat. All were quietly fanning themselves. Ian waved and called out friendly greetings to most of them.

The first house on the right sported a small store in front. The old, faded sign on the door stated that it was open. The older couple lounging nearby watched them closely.

She attracted attention, she could tell. By now, everyone probably knew she'd plunged her car into the water. It was like that in small communities. There were no secrets.

"What do most of these people do for a living?" she asked Ian quietly as they walked down the dirt road.

"Some fish. A few are artisans, making hand-made souvenirs for tourists." He swatted away a mosquito. "But most are unemployed. 'The Shepherd's Smile' will change the lifestyle here. Change it for the better. I know it."

"It hasn't already?"

"It's new. The Vincentis have hired me to implement it. Both are good Christians who can see beyond the poverty and the blame that gets tossed around and are willing to do something to help these people."

They slowed where the road curled into a cul-de-sac. "What are their plans?" she asked.

"First up was to plant a church and let God reach these people."

They stopped at one of the trailers on the right. Rusting in several streaks, it sat parallel to the dirt road. In front sat a small garden of tomatoes and peppers. Several banana palms and one orange tree offered a bit of shade to its side deck, which was met by a tidy path of white rocks and crushed shells. All over the place, potted geraniums and other heat-loving flowers nodded in the light breeze. Liz could smell their blossoms from the road.

A loud, squawking sound sliced through the hot air. With bright colors, a bird flashed past them, startling Liz.

Charlie laughed. "It's Joseph, Auntie Liz! He's come to say hello!"

Ian took her arm to steady her. "Joseph is named for his colorful coat. He's our local runaway and has been around for years. We think he's a rainbow lorikeet that escaped from someone's home in Northglade. He follows people around. Everyone likes him except Elsie, who says he's always pecking at her plants just to annoy her."

The bird landed on the small side deck in front of them, cocked his head and said something unintelligible.

"Shoo, you crazy bird! You're always getting where you don't belong. Shoo!" The voice continued, "Come in! We've been waiting too long with this meal, and George says he won't wait any longer." A tall, strong woman exited the trailer. She stopped when she spotted Liz. Her short, frizzy gray hair stuck out in all directions, and her dark skin bore a sheen of perspiration.

She turned to Ian and set her hands on her hips. "You could have told me we were having company."

"I'm sorry, Elsie. I only just found out. This is Liz Tate, Charlie's aunt."

Her frown deepening, Elsie wiped her hands on her apron and trotted down the steps. Over the hot breeze, Liz listened to the woman's footfalls crunching on the shell walkway. Elsie stuck out her hand toward Liz. "Charlie's aunt, you say? I didn't know he had one. Not that the boy talked any."

"He can, though," Ian answered blandly. "He used my cell to call Liz, who figured out where we were."

After shooting Ian a questioning frown, Elsie lifted her graying eyebrows. "Well, come inside. I haven't got a fancy air conditioner, but I do have a gallon of cold lemonade and a good fan."

Ahead of them, Charlie galloped up the stairs and disappeared into the mobile home. He reappeared a moment later with a cell phone and shoved it toward Ian.

"Thank you," Charlie said. "I'm sorry I used all the battery, but I didn't wreck it. Honest."

Ian nodded. Liz thought he might be holding his breath, hoping for more from the boy, but no more words came.

"Elsie," he asked, "we've had a dip in the water. Is it all right if Liz has a shower here? I'll run home for one and be back in ten minutes."

"I'm afraid I'll need more than a shower," Liz told the woman. "I don't have any dry clothes."

"That's no trouble. I have something that'll fit you." Elsie led them into the front room where she told her husband to pull another chair up to the kitchen table and that supper would be ready as soon as Liz showered and Ian returned.

A good wash and a clean dress felt good, Liz decided after she was done. Though the dress was simple and long—and identical to the one Monica wore—Liz was grateful.

Thank you, Lord.

She walked into the small trailer's kitchen just as Ian opened the side door and entered.

His hair was still damp and finger-combed, his clothes lightweight and crisp. Liz found herself staring at him, all fresh and clean, his expression so full of concern and compassion. He smiled at her. And automatically, her heart tripped up. To cover her sudden fluster, she looked away.

Ian walked over to George as he pulled up a fifth chair to the small round table. He spoke quietly, with Liz catching only a few words: a tropical storm coming, George telling Ian not to overwork himself and feel free to ask others to help.

It would appear that George was part of this whole Witness Security Program. And probably Elsie, too. Liz didn't know enough to make any more assumptions than that.

She caught more of Ian's words. He had called his supervisor, suggesting Charlie be moved immediately, but his supervisor disagreed.

Liz stared at Ian, openly eavesdropping because this was too important for any good manners. The supervisor ordered them to stay put, to see who might show up, that he and the Wilsons were well trained for this. And extra help was on its way.

And judging by George's deepening frown, Liz would guess he didn't like that answer any more than Ian did.

Someone might show up? Hadn't Ian hinted of that when they were talking in the clinic? If he suspected as much, then he must have told his supervisor. Now, with George talking about a tropical storm coming and Charlie being used as bait, she knew only one thing.

Charlie shouldn't be here, no matter how well trained anyone was or how much extra help was on its way.

"I should go, as soon as possible," she said after George gave thanks for their meal of hearty sandwiches and crisp salad. "There are a hundred reasons why I should take Charlie and leave. Including your workload, that tropical storm coming and the fact that someone might be here—" she glanced at Charlie, who was busy removing the green peppers from his salad "—ahead of me."

Ian set down his fork. "Charlie is safest with me."

"You need to pastor these people, too. I heard what George said. You can only spread yourself out so thin."

"You should let me worry about that."

"And," Elsie added, pouring more lemonade, "you two need to talk about it down in his office." She shot Charlie a quick look. Having dissected his food, he was happy to crunch on the carrots he'd found in his salad. He appeared to be ignoring both of them.

"There's nothing to discuss," Ian answered calmly. "A taxi won't come down this far from Northglade. You may not realize that it's only a small town itself, with not much in it."

She'd seen Northglade on the map, a community inland from Spring Island with a farm population. She doubted there were any motels there.

"Are you saying you won't let me go?"

He leaned forward. He'd chosen a seat across the table from her and now drilled a stare into her. "You've been traveling for how long? You had a scare and a dunk in the water, and you haven't slept since Saturday night, I'd guess. It would be very wise to spend the night here. If the Wilsons will have you."

"Of course we will." Elsie nodded. "Liz, dear, even if you could find a car to get you off the island, do you think you should be driving after all you've been through? I can see it in your eyes, just how tired you are. And I know you don't want to risk Charlie's life because of a little stubbornness."

She'd expected some manipulation out of Charlie, because he was just a child and they sometimes did that sort of thing, but she hadn't expected it out of the adults around the table.

But they were right. More than right. She was practically dead on her feet. Ian hit the nail on the head when he said she hadn't slept. The evening Charlie had called, she'd been up arranging flights until the wee hours. The next day she flew out and then spent that night waiting for a connecting flight at Newark. Was it Wednesday already? And she hadn't slept since Saturday night?

The reminder of that fact brought a yawn to her jaw, something she stifled quickly.

"Stay the night here, Liz," Ian said quietly. "It's the best thing."

"But what about—" Still holding her glass of lemonade she dropped her voice "—whoever might be here?"

"Let me worry about that. You need to sleep, and we can discuss anything in the morning."

She stared into his eyes, feeling the pull of that attraction again. A man who had given up a career to serve God. A man who cared enough for Charlie to risk his life. A handsome, compelling, intelligent man. Whose brilliant blue eyes met hers with a magnetism she couldn't pull away from.

You've found Charlie. He's safe. Rest tonight. Get some sleep.

Logic told her to capitulate. But she couldn't ignore all that Ian had said back at the rec center. Charlie was in danger. The man who'd killed Jerry would come after him.

And yet, despite the fear rising in her again, she read Ian's clear expression.

Trust me.

She took a shaky sip of her drink. *Should I, Lord?*

"We'll put a cot in Charlie's room. He can sleep on it, and Liz can have his bed." Oblivious to Liz's warring thoughts, Elsie settled the matter with a firm nod.

"Liz," Ian added softly, "we'll talk about it tomorrow. In the meantime, get some rest. It's really the best thing."

Fatigue rolled over her in one heavy, blanketing wave. Elsie had kept her curtains closed, and only through the tiny window above the sink did Liz see that night was closing fast.

With all eyes on her, Liz fought off the weariness. "Okay. And I bet I won't be long in bed after Charlie."

"Dad said I don't have to go to bed early," Charlie piped up.

Elsie arched her eyebrows at him. "If it was a school night you'd be going to bed early, young man."

Charlie's bottom lip pushed forward slightly. "Dad said I don't need school. He said that I'm smart."

Liz frowned at him. "Then you're smart enough to know that you need your rest." With that, she pulled out his chair and stood tiredly. "And you're smart enough to know we should help Elsie do the dishes."

As they rounded the table, she caught Elsie peering knowingly at her husband. "I told you he could talk just fine."

George snorted. "Talking to his aunt ain't the talking he should be doin', and you know it, Elsie."

* * *

Ian said his good-nights a short time later, thanking Elsie as he always did, for all she was doing for him and Charlie.

At the door, the older woman patted his arm. "You're more than welcome, and don't worry about a thing. Everything will work out. You just need faith, that's all."

She'd taken one look at him when he'd shown up for supper and guessed his thoughts. Yes, he was busy right now. Too busy, and Liz's arrival didn't make things any easier. Quite the opposite, in fact. He'd called his supervisor in DC to inform him that she'd not only shown up but had also claimed she'd been run off the road. Ian had wanted to berate the man for not telling him about her, but all his supervisor had said was she had no claim on Charlie and wouldn't be a problem. Ian reminded him that she'd seen her nephew regularly enough to have the boy call her the second he got to a phone, but the man refused to admit his mistake.

Suppressing a yawn, Ian rubbed his face. He felt like something the cat dragged in. While George liked to stay up late, watching TV until after midnight, Ian napped in the evening and spent the rest of the night next door, working on the program the Vincentis had hired him to implement, all the while watching the Wilson trailer.

Those short bouts of sleep were catching up with him. He hadn't expected any trouble before Liz showed up, and now that Charlie's location was compromised, sleep would be even more elusive.

Ian's supervisor wanted Charlie to remain on the island as bait. And with the storm coming, all flights were cancelled, all roads plugged with residents already leaving, going to fully booked hotels inland. Most of the villagers here couldn't afford that luxury and would wait until the shelters opened. Getting Charlie off the island would be easy. Finding a place for him much harder. And he needed Liz to go, too, or Charlie might sink back into his silence again.

He sighed, knowing he couldn't fool himself. There was another reason for not wanting to have Charlie and Liz removed, and Ian knew it. He'd never given up on a case. He'd never been removed from a case. He'd been one hundred percent successful at cases worse than this one.

Ian trudged into his house, not bothering with the lights, even though night had fallen. He lived next door to the Wilsons, and on the other side was the Callahan house. Stephen Callahan, one of several boys just a bit younger than Charlie, had latched on to the boy as a playmate. But tonight, their house was dark. Leo Callahan had managed to secure work at the resort's work site as a general laborer. The work was hard in this heat, so Ian wasn't surprised to see all the windows open.

There were no streetlights in Moss Point. Down the road, the rec center had a security light out front, for all the good it did, with the dense foliage between the building and the rest of the village. From where Ian stood, he could see the bugs flying in and out of the light's glowing circle, thick enough to look like snow swirling on a winter's evening back home in Virginia.

He'd seen plenty of snow the winter that came to mind. He'd taken off from his uncle's house. Uncle Ed hadn't wanted his younger brother's bad kid, and that winter, Ian had had enough of the abuse. The snow that night had been thick, flying past the streetlights as Ian had walked the town until dawn.

Shaking off the unpleasant memories, Ian looked out at the middle window, just past the small deck. A blurry silhouette walked past the high, small window. Liz was preparing for bed. A moment later, the light winked out.

He turned away, flopped onto his couch and shut his eyes.

Something jerked him awake.

A yell. A loud and insistent dog barking. A glance at his watch told him that two hours had passed. He then looked over at the front window, thinking it odd to see a flickering, orange glow outside.

He leaped up. A house was on fire!

FIVE

The Wilsons! Ian bolted out the door, his gaze shooting to the house on his left. But their small home was quiet and dark. Ian spun around.

The Callahans! Leo was running outside, dropping a small child on the ground out front. He turned and raced back in the door. Ian tore across the thin, scruffy lawn to snatch the little girl, Stephen's younger sister, away to safety.

By then, Elsie was hurrying along the road, her housecoat flapping. Ian shoved the child in her arms. He practically ran into Leo on his way through the door. This time the man carried a sleepy Stephen in his arms.

"Who else is in here? Where's Jenny?" Ian asked.

At that moment, Jenny appeared at the door. Ian took Stephen in his arms, tossing the boy over his shoulder. At the same time, he pulled Jenny Callahan away from the house.

"It's in the back bedroom!" Leo gasped out. He had an oddly deep voice for a skinny man. "That's where it started!"

Jenny grabbed her son. Elsie came close, still holding her daughter, and pulled the mother and child away from the house.

"I've got a hose," Ian called out. "Someone call the fire department."

"Already done," George said, hurrying up. "Elsie, get into the house with Jenny and the kids. Lock the doors, and don't come out!"

Ian's thoughts exactly. He'd been a marshal for too long to see this fire as a coincidence. Sure, it was two houses down from the Wilsons, but it could also be a ruse. Something to get everyone busy while the real target was sought.

William Smith, the man suspected of murdering Jerry Troop, could be using this to empty the Wilsons' house.

Elsie was already on her deck steps, with Jenny close behind her. They herded Stephen, who was now awake and walking, into the house. With a relieved sigh, Ian caught a glimpse of Charlie at the threshold, before Elsie guided him into the house and shut the door. The commotion must have woken him up, but Ian was glad for it.

Ian hurried over to the side of his house where a battered hose was wound over an old truck rim bolted to his house. He'd been on the island over five months and had yet to use it. The tap squeaked as he wrenched on it, but thankfully, water spat out the end. Leo grabbed it and ran, nearly plowing into Monica, who'd appeared suddenly with an empty bucket. Her house was on the other side of the Callahans, and judging from the drips of water in the bucket, she'd already tossed its contents on the fire.

With a rake he found in his backyard, Ian hooked and then tore off the bedroom window's screen, noticing that it was already ripped. Then he grabbed the hose and began to spray down the interior of the house. Thick black smoke with a smell of gas to it rolled out and upward.

"Monica, fill up your bucket again!" he yelled.

She raced away, leaving him to spray the fire as best he could. Water on a gasoline fire. Not the best choice, he knew, but the only one right now.

George and Leo had found buckets of their own and were tossing water into the window. Ian had no idea how they managed to fill them so quickly, unless they'd run down the short trail between the Wilsons' and his house to the old dock and scooped out gulf water.

The whole time, Poco, the Callahans' excitable mutt, barked and bayed wildly, prancing around. Ian heard Leo yell at him and chase him off, and a moment later, he could hear Jenny calling to the dog. The barking stopped, and a door slammed. Jenny must have brought the dog into the Wilsons' house.

Ian thought of Liz, wondering if she was awake. Why she wasn't out here helping. He'd pegged her as that kind of person.

The smoke slowed down, a strong sizzling reaching their ears, and Ian dared to hope that they had the fire under control.

"The bed is still burning," Leo panted out. "It was the only thing on fire when I first noticed it."

"It's good you're all safe," Ian answered, still spraying.

"We were sleeping in the living room. It's the coolest place in the house."

"Whose bedroom is that?"

"Jenny's and mine." He grimaced at the open window, where smoke no longer poured outward. "We had all the windows open, too, to catch a breeze. It's the only way to stay cool."

Monica came up close after throwing another bucket of water into the window. Ian knew the dangers of going inside to continue to fight the fire, but with the nearest fire department at least half an hour away in Northglade, they couldn't just stand there and spray from the outside. And if the mattress continued to burn inside the house…

He handed the hose to Monica. "Keep spraying through the window. Come on, Leo, let's get that mattress outside."

Thankfully, the mattress was no longer smoldering. They managed to drag it outside where Monica hosed it down thoroughly. Bedding and clothes in the room, plus a few small pieces of furniture, were tossed out the window. And finally, it seemed everything was under control.

Ian pulled the mattress farther away from the house, leaving Leo and Monica to flip and move the other items around in search of hot spots. He was about twenty feet from the house when he heard Monica's soft voice carry through the warm air.

"Don't ask me again. I won't."

Leo said something deep and indiscernible in return. Then they immediately stopped and looked over at Ian. Standing beside the mattress, he could easily smell the petroleum products in the air but waited until Leo walked up to him.

"What were you doing to start this fire?" he asked Leo.

"Nothing. Like I said, we were all sleeping in the living room. I need to sleep. The work at the resort is hard."

At some point George had turned on Ian's outside light, and in that light, Ian could see Leo's face scrunch into a furious frown. Monica had slipped close, too, he noticed.

"Leo, can you smell the gas?"

Leo looked up, his gaze skimming past Monica's nervous one. Ian watched both people swallow. Finally, Leo spoke. "I can now that you mention it. What does it mean? I don't own a car, and I don't have oil in the house. I didn't do this."

"Do you use any oil at work?"

"No, but it's a construction site! There's probably some there, but we've been installing solar panels the last few days. Except that work has been put aside because of the storm. The foreman wants to wait until they figure out if it's coming this way or not."

Again, his eyes roamed over to Monica's. Ian caught her wetting her lips and stepping back.

Ian bent down and peered at the mattress. A shard of smoke-darkened glass could be seen embedded in the outer cover. Flakes of burned cotton disintegrated when he poked them with the rake.

A Molotov cocktail. A crude, yet effective way to set a fire. And the screen had already been ripped, he'd noticed.

No, not ripped, he remembered, but rather sliced through quite neatly like with a sharp knife.

Leo moved away, toeing the charred and soaking remains of his bedroom, bending occasionally to pick something up.

"Someone threw gas on the mattress?" Monica asked. "Why—" Immediately, she shut her mouth.

Again, Ian caught the nervous silent exchange between the two neighbors. Then everyone went quiet.

"Do you think the fire's out?" Monica finally asked timidly.

"I'd say, but we'll wait for the fire department to tell us for sure."

"I'll leave then."

Ian looked at her. "Did you hear Leo yelling?"

"Um, yes, I think so. Or maybe it was the dog. I don't remember." She glanced around before moving away.

Ian watched her, noting how she still wore that simple dress she's worn the previous day when he'd been pulling Liz from the sinking car. She'd found the time to throw it on, which in itself wasn't suspicious, but, as she turned away from him, he noted that her hair was still piled high in the same messy bun she wore before, revealing the dress's clasp at the nape of the neck.

She'd managed to fasten that clasp, too, something he wouldn't have considered to be that important, unless she hadn't even gone to bed. It had to be after 1:00 a.m.

The hairs on his scalp tingled, a sure sign to him that something wasn't right.

"How's everyone at your house?" he asked George, who'd stopped beside him.

"Fine. Elsie got the kids back to sleep, and she and Jenny have made a pitcher of iced tea." George wiped his forehead with a faded handkerchief. "I expect we'll be up for the rest of the night. The police and the fire department are still about fifteen minutes away."

"And Liz?"

"You were bang on right when you said she was tired. She hasn't woken up yet, even with Elsie putting the two boys in Charlie's room with her."

It was a small mercy that she hadn't driven away with Charlie tonight. Sure, she hadn't been offered a car, but should she have found one, like his SUV now parked behind his house, she'd have been a danger to herself and Charlie.

Ian pivoted quietly, his words for George alone. "Someone deliberately set this fire."

"I guessed as much, considering the smell of gas."

"But Leo and his family were in the living room tonight because it was cooler than the bedrooms."

"So someone who didn't know that tried to kill him and his family? Or do you think Leo did this to himself?"

"I was thinking it might have also been a diversion."

"It didn't work. Perhaps because of Poco. He's big enough and loud enough to scare off anyone."

Ian glanced around. From his view through the trees in the Callahans' small backyard, he could see Monica opening her own back door. With a hasty glance over at Leo, she hurried inside her house. "And there's something going on between Leo and Monica. They seemed pretty nervous around each other."

George peeked over his shoulder. "I don't know why. Except…"

"Except what?" Ian asked.

He pondered his answer first, then finally said, "Except that Monica is heavily in debt. I don't know who she borrowed money from, but I'd say it wasn't from the banks. I do know she owes thousands of dollars and hasn't paid anything back yet. She told Elsie at the women's Bible study that she needs to make money fast. She was asking what she might do to get some fast cash."

Ian clenched his jaw, noting that both the Callahan house and Monica's were nearly identical, both bungalows having been built during some distant boom time.

Great. Another suspicion. The fire might have been a ruse to lure them away from Charlie, but it could have also been a mistake. Whoever Monica had borrowed money from could have been looking for their payment or putting pressure on her to cough it up.

Though Liz's dark, curly hair wasn't like Monica's medium-brown waves, they were both the same approximate age. Had Liz been mistaken for Monica when she'd been run off the road?

Did that mean that Smith wasn't on the island after all?

No, Ian refused to slacken his vigilance because of a supposition.

Hours later, after the fire department had arrived and the house was checked completely, the police report filled out and the mattress taken away by them, Ian trudged into the Wilsons' house.

Leo and Jenny had taken their daughter and were staying at a friend's house at the end of the road, while Elsie kept Stephen, the little boy who'd befriended Charlie.

"How are the boys?" he asked Elsie, accepting a tall glass of iced tea.

"Fine. Sleeping like babies."

"And Liz?"

"She didn't wake up. That poor woman was dead on her feet, though she didn't know it until her head hit the pillow. And you look pretty battered as well."

He smiled at her, thankful that Liz had stayed zonked out. She'd use this incident to walk off the island with Charlie, he was sure.

Elsie's front room curtains hung slightly ajar, and dawn was peeking through the eastern trees, a pink and dark orange glow that warned of bad weather ahead.

A noise down the hall made both of them turn. Liz was coming out, wearing the dress that Elsie had given her. It was identical to the one Monica wore last night, and only then did he remember that Elsie had made the women in the village two simple dresses each. She'd been given bolts of different patterned material, and running off the same pattern of dress was probably as easy for the woman as cooking up a pot of seafood bisque or a plate of hush puppies.

"What's going on? There's some boy sleeping on the floor beside Charlie. Well, he's not now. I set him up onto the bed." She looked from Elsie to Ian. "What's wrong?"

"The Callahans, the family beside my house, had a fire last night. Stephen Callahan is the boy in your room."

Liz gasped. "Is everyone okay?"

"They're all fine. Just the back bedroom was damaged, but thankfully they were all sleeping in the living room. Leo Callahan said it was cooler there."

"I'll get some coffee on." Elsie walked into the kitchen.

Liz touched Ian's arm. He smelled like smoke but hoped she wouldn't notice. Or at least not notice that the smoke bore the oily hint of burning fuel. "How does this affect Charlie?" she asked.

"We need to talk about that, but first, I need other answers." He walked into the kitchen, with Liz on his heels. "Elsie, did Monica ever mention to you that she was in debt?"

Looking up from her coffee canister, Elsie wore a shocked expression. "You know I shouldn't talk about what we women say at our Bible study, Ian. It's wrong to gossip."

"It's not gossip. I'm trying to think of a reason someone would set fire to the Callahans' house."

"Monica wouldn't do that!"

"I'm thinking that someone targeted the wrong house."

Elsie gasped. "You think that some loan shark tried to threaten Monica but got the Callahans' house? Could it be that dangerous?"

"It all depends on where she borrowed the money from. Why do you think it was a loan shark?"

Elsie bit her lip, her brow wrinkling in worry. "She said she needed money right away and that she'd borrowed some and the people wanted it back now. She said they refused to wait, and though she didn't admit it, I think she was scared of them.

But she didn't say why she borrowed the money or who from." She shook her head. "That's all I know, Ian, and don't ask me anything more. This is horrible."

"Why would Monica borrow money in the first place?" Liz asked. "What's her lifestyle like?"

"The same as ours," Ian answered. "Which makes it odd that she needs money because she hasn't spent in a way that shows here."

"You hired her," Liz pointed out, glancing at Elsie as the older woman looked deep in thought. "Did she say how she was going to spend her wages?"

"Like everyone else, on bills," Elsie answered quickly, putting away the coffee canister. "We all have bills, and Monica was complaining once how much groceries cost. She asked me the other day about starting a garden."

Liz's expression went distant.

Only when silence dropped on them did Ian notice her concern. "What's wrong?" Ian asked.

"I just realized something. When did this fire start?"

"Around midnight. The police and fire department left about a half hour ago."

Her words hollow sounding, she said, "I slept through it all?"

"Honey, you were exhausted," Elsie said, pouring coffee. "You'd have slept even if a brass band paraded through that bedroom. Ha! With that dog and those boys, I think the noise was the same."

Absently, Liz accepted a cup of coffee and walked around the counter to the table. She sank into a chair, her eyes hollow. "I must have been really tired. That's awful. I came so close to leaving last night. I had planned to leave if I'd had my rental. Think of how dangerous that would have been."

"But you didn't," Ian answered, sitting down beside her.

"You're certain that the fire was started by some loan shark looking to collect?" she asked him.

Ian took a sip of coffee. "I don't know. It was just a suggestion. There was a smell of gasoline to the fire, and the police suspect it was deliberately set. But we can't rule anything out."

She set down her coffee mug. "This isn't a safe place for Charlie anymore. Even you have to admit that."

Ian folded his arms. He didn't have to admit anything. "Look, Liz, this may not have anything to do with Charlie."

"But you won't rule it out, either. Ian, I need to take Charlie and leave. That's the only way."

"Not without a marshal, and even if we called right now, another one wouldn't be available immediately."

"What about you?"

"Look, Liz, you're both safer here. All the roads are jammed with people leaving, and all the hotels are booked solid. George and Elsie and I can handle the security better here."

"Security? You're going to use Charlie as bait!" She tightened her jaw.

"Apprehending Jerry's killer is crucial to saving thousands of lives. We can lure him out without endangering Charlie. But if we move off the island into the general population, with no immediate destination, we risk not only our own lives but innocent strangers' lives, too."

"Why isn't there another marshal on his way, if this is so dangerous?"

"Things take time to happen. The nearest marshal office is in Miami."

He felt Liz study him. Her eyes had narrowed slightly, and it didn't take a psychiatrist to figure out she didn't like him. And why should she? He'd taken Charlie and refused to give him up, telling her what she should do even.

The coffee he'd just swallowed sat like molten lead in his stomach. *She doesn't understand,* he told himself.

"We need to get off this island, Ian. Someone ran me off the road, and someone set fire to a nearby house. We don't know if they have anything to do with Charlie being here or not. I do know that these incidents could be proof that Charlie is in danger. This village is no longer safe for him."

"You're not leaving until I say so."

She straightened, and her voice rose. "You can't stop us."

He spoke back just as sharply. "I can and I will."

Liz set down her coffee cup and opened her mouth again. But before she could speak, Elsie plunked her hands down between them and drilled a dark glare at the arguing pair. "Look, you two, you both want Charlie safe, but you aren't going to sort this out here, and I won't have you waking up those two boys with your arguing. You need to discuss this, yes, but take it down to Ian's office. You'll be able to make the arrangements from there and shout at each other all you want, too." She finished off her censure with an added glare at each of them.

Ian sat back. Elsie was right. He was exhausted, and irritation grated on him more than he realized. He drew in a breath to restore his self-control and nodded. "Yes, we should talk in my office. Let me grab a shower and a couple hours' sleep. It's too early to call anyone anyway."

Liz blinked and frowned and then agreed with a nod of her own. With a stiff rise and stretch, Ian walked to the door. "Liz, I know it's hard for you to believe, but I do want what's best for Charlie."

Her own frown continued as he left.

Two hours later, Ian stopped by the Wilsons' to take Liz to his office. He'd grabbed a pretty good nap after a shower. He'd made a coffee and a sandwich and was now better prepared to talk to her. He'd expected the boys to stay sleeping, but when he arrived, Charlie was up, finishing his cereal. And he wanted to stay with Liz.

The three of them walked outside in an uneasy silence. Liz broke it when she asked, "Which house was it?"

"That one." He pointed to the Callahans' house. From the front, it looked normal. The rear was charred and burned. Though it was 8:30 in the morning, the village was quiet. Poco, the dog, was sniffing around the house, but when he spotted Ian and Liz, he didn't bark. The Callahans didn't mind letting the dog roam, and Jenny must have let him out sometime during the early morning.

They made their way down to the rec center, Ian unlocking the building and then his office. Liz followed him in, watching him walk around to the other side of the desk to pick up the phone.

"Are you two going to fight?" Charlie asked. He blinked innocently at Liz, and Ian watched as she returned the smile with a melting one of her own, her arms opening to let the boy walk into them.

He climbed up onto her lap. Being a small, agile boy, he looked like he'd done this a thousand times before.

"Ian is going to see about us leaving," Liz said quietly.

"Me, too?"

"Yes."

Ian grimaced. Liz must have caught the twist in his mouth because she added, "No promises one way or another. He's just going to make some phone calls."

"To the marshal people?"

"Yes," Ian answered tersely. He didn't like how much Charlie noticed things around him. But Jerry Troop had been right about one thing. The kid was smart. No wonder Liz was able to locate the boy. He noticed everything and could articulate better than Ian realized.

With a shake of his head, he let his gaze shift around the room to land on the credenza.

The light on his printer was blinking. He glanced down at the paper tray at the bottom of the printer. Empty.

He hadn't printed out anything since before Vacation Bible School began a week ago. Why was his printer on now? What was waiting in the print queue?

After walking over to his computer, where he confirmed it had been improperly shut down, he turned it on. Then, after grabbing paper from a new bundle in the cupboard of the credenza, he shoved a short stack into the tray. Without hesitation, he hit the resume button.

"What's wrong?" Liz asked, with Charlie on her lap.

"I don't know. I don't remember leaving this printer on, especially in the out of paper mode." He looked up at her, feeling his brows furrow. "There's something in the printer's memory. Someone printed out something then ran out of paper and left it."

"Maybe Monica. You said she's helping you here."

"Maybe." By now, the printer had responded, spitting out printed paper at a speed he knew would use the minimal amount of ink in the shortest time.

He picked up the first few pages. After setting Charlie on his feet, Liz came up close to him and looked down as well. She gasped. "It's about Charlie!"

SIX

Ice crawled up Liz's spine, spreading over the nape of her neck to make her curls feel as though they were standing straight up. The paper in Ian's hand was part of a marshal report on Charlie. Everything a person would need to know about him, including hints on how to gain the boy's trust. Ian picked up the last sheet. It was a memorandum on Jerry's death with scribbling on the bottom right corner: "Suspect child of witnessing murder. Acquire statement at all costs."

"Whoa," she whispered through her horror. "Why do you…what reason would you have to get this… stuff? You said you were once a marshal, but *all* of this? A personality profile? Advice on gaining his trust?" Her jumbled words died away, and she found she could no longer speak.

Ian ignored her. He scooped up the remaining papers, one even out of Liz's hands before unlocking his filing cabinet. A moment later, he'd pulled a file from the top drawer and tucked all of the sheets into the light brown folder. Then he slammed shut the drawer and locked it again. After that, he sat at his computer.

"What's going on, Ian? Why did you print this out?"

He said nothing, and with tightened shoulders, she walked around his desk to stand behind him and openly read his computer. She didn't care if it was an invasion of privacy. This was about Charlie, and anything involving him involved her, too.

Ian was flipping through files in various programs back and forth and checking his printer record all too quickly for her to read. He wrote down a date and time and quickly exited all the programs.

"Talk to me, Ian. I need to know if this is about Charlie and—"

"Someone accessed my computer and printed out confidential files. I had password-protected them and hadn't even printed them out myself. I'd only read them on the computer. Someone tried to print them out but was cut short for some reason, probably running out of time and paper. They took what they had and left in a hurry."

Liz grabbed Ian's arm. She pressed him. "Who would be able to get this information? Who has keys to this office and knows your password? Talk to me, Ian. Do you think this has anything to do with that fire last night? This all affects Charlie, remember?"

She waited for him to answer, impatiently filled with fear for Charlie. Her hand still rested on Ian's warm arm. She could smell his clean scent. She could feel the concern emanate from him along with a host of complicated feelings.

And slowly came the complete and obvious understanding that regardless of how attractive she found Ian, regardless of how much he cared for Charlie, he was someone she needed to stay far away from. For Charlie's sake. She needed to remain calm, in control, trustworthy and focused on helping Charlie heal. She wouldn't get that hanging around Ian.

And on the heels of that reaction nipped disappointment. Almost as strong as the fear and dread.

"It was Monica."

Both Ian and Liz turned to Charlie. The boy still sat on the chair, his eyes wide behind the glasses that Liz wanted to rip off his face and stomp on. "Monica? Why do you say that?" she asked him. "Did you see her?"

"No."

"Then how do you know she printed anything out?"

Charlie shrugged. "I saw her go back into Ian's office when she told him about you falling into the water. Then she came down the road to where Auntie Liz's car was."

"When we were on the causeway?"

He nodded. "When Ian told me to stand near the sign. She came up to me, and she had something shoved in her dress. Dad would sometimes put stuff down his pants and have to hold it there cuz it would fall out."

Liz swallowed. She didn't dare ask what his father would put there. Jerry had been as thin as a rail, a man whose jeans were always baggy. If he'd shoved drugs in his pants, they'd surely fall down his pant leg. She stole a fast look at Ian.

"How do you know she had something in her dress?" Ian asked calmly. "She wouldn't show you."

Charlie giggled, a sweet sound so totally out of place for the situation, but being a young boy, he'd find the whole notion silly. "Course not. But a couple of papers fell out, and she hid them in the woods. I bet she took the papers from here. She always looks over your shoulder when you're at the computer."

Beside Ian, Liz peered down at him. She should rely on his expertise here, but every part of her was screaming that she should leave with Charlie now and forget about all of these people.

Abruptly, the phone rang. Ian turned away from her, his eyebrows close together as he reached for the telephone on his desk. "Hello?"

He listened closely, grabbing a pen and paper. He scribbled down something and then turned to the computer.

When he'd hung up, he looked up at her. "The tropical storm that's east of the Yucatan is increasing in strength. They expect it to become a hurricane by tonight. And it's supposed to move eastward."

"What does that mean?"

"Everything to us. Evacuations, preparations for that." He ran his fingers through his hair. Hadn't George warned him last night about having too much responsibility?

Yes, one more reason to leave. "May I borrow your phone? I'd like to order another car."

"They won't deliver one until after the storm."

"Let them tell me that."

Liz slipped in behind the desk. A few minutes later, the rental agency said they couldn't deliver another car until after the storm. Ian was right and had allowed her to discover that for herself. She needed to trust him more.

And no sooner had she set down the phone did it ring again.

Ian answered it, and after hanging up, he said, "That was the tow truck. He's almost to the causeway." He glanced over at Charlie.

Liz read his thoughts. "I'll take Charlie back to the Wilsons' house, and then we'll go." She stood and took the boy's hand. "We'll talk about leaving later. We may even be able to get a ride with the tow truck driver."

Before he could contradict her, she and Charlie walked out of his office.

Ten minutes later, she met Ian in front of the rec center.

"The driver is at the causeway, waiting for us," he said tersely. "He called after I'd finished telling my supervisor about Monica."

And my desire to leave, Liz thought.

They hurried down to the causeway in time to see the driver's assistant standing on the rocks, hook in hand, looking grimly down at the water. He wore a wet suit but no goggles. His face was flushed and sweating in the heat of the morning.

After speaking to the driver who stood near the bumper, the younger man waded into the water. He dipped down under the water and resurfaced a moment later without the hook.

Liz watched, held her breath without knowing why and all the while berated herself for the unsettling feeling. It wasn't as if there was a body slopping about in there. Though it felt like that.

Yuck. She'd watched too many crime shows on TV.

At the front bumper, the driver picked up the winch control and took up the slack. With sickening groans of suction and scraping, the rental car slowly emerged, hood first. The driver parked it on the rocks to drain it.

Ian walked around the back of the truck, and Liz followed. When they reached the far side, Liz stopped and gasped.

The whole side of her car was scraped. Long blue streaks started from the mirror, which was now dangling, all the way to the rear bumper. Her rental was red. The blue stood out starkly.

Crossing her arms, she shivered, despite the heat of another sweltering day. The driver told them he was going to turn around and back in to hoist the car up and over the remaining rocks, before he towed it away. To the police station, he added after pointing to the scrapes on the side.

"But first, I'll drain it all completely. And check for snakes," he added.

"Snakes?" Liz echoed.

"Yup. Got them old water moccasins here and they can be nasty. That's why my guy's wearing that suit. He doesn't like to get bit, and those snakes are mean. We'll drain the car and see if any of them hitched a ride."

Liz shot a shocked look at Ian. "You have poisonous snakes here?"

"Relax. We have traps all over the place. Under the rec center are at least four of them."

"Traps? How good are they?"

"They work. But don't forget, water moccasins like to live in water, hence their name."

"Not all the time," the guy in the wet suit called over his shoulder.

Liz blinked at Ian as he led them out of the other men's earshot. "And have you told Charlie about all of this? He's a typical kid, and no-doubt will want to catch a snake. Ian, this place isn't safe."

"It will have to be, Liz, because you can't leave. You have no car until after the storm, and I won't let you leave without a marshal."

"Who won't come before the storm, either, I suppose." She shoved her hands on her hips.

"Liz, this is all for your own safety and Charlie's. Why can't you accept that?"

"Charlie's safety means more to me than my life. It's just that you're busy doing a laundry list of things. You can't look after Charlie in the way you say he deserves. So why are you being so adamant about keeping him here?" She paused, drew in a breath, and opened her mouth slightly in understanding. "It's not his safety, and it's not just so he can finger his dad's killer. You don't want him to leave because that would be a failure on your part.

They reinstated you as a marshal, and if you fail now that would make you look really bad, wouldn't it?"

Ian looked away, and Liz pursed her lips. She knew immediately that she'd struck a nerve.

He wanted to succeed. Maybe he had a perfect record, or maybe he'd failed the U.S. Marshal Service in some way, perhaps by leaving before retirement.

It didn't matter to her. Nobody's pride or feeling of self-worth mattered while Charlie's life was in danger. Nobody's. Not even her own.

She turned to watch the assistant open the car doors and the trunk. The driver pulled up on the chain to tip the back end down, allowing more murky water to cascade back into the inlet.

Tears sprang to her eyes. Someone had wanted her dead. They didn't want her to take Charlie. Could it be Jerry's killer? Was he already here on Spring Island?

She walked over to the driver. "Excuse me? Is it possible for you to take me into Northglade? Is there a car rental place there?"

"Sorry, I can't do that. Company policy. Insurance stuff, I think. But your rental company should bring you a new car."

"Not until after the storm, I'm afraid."

The driver checked the sky. "Oh, the one heading over this way. I bet you'll have to evacuate this place. Isn't there a resort being built here? Maybe they've got someone who's leaving this place?"

Liz sagged. "I'll look into it. Thanks."

Ian heard her request. He was still bristling from her cool remarks about how he didn't want to fail. Truth hurts, all right. He'd had a perfect record, and if Liz or Charlie became injured or they were forced to leave, it wouldn't look good on him.

He hated that he'd even have that thought. He shouldn't be so selfish. Nor should he be blaming Liz for her keen observation.

He wiped his face and shoved his hat farther down on his head. Liz didn't know the details surrounding Jerry's death. Charlie could identify William Smith, and with his statement, they could bring down many evil people. A whole cartel could theoretically be eliminated, reducing the flow of drugs into this country by a considerable percentage. That would save lives, more than "The Shepherd's Smile," right?

Ian blew out a long breath. Was he meant to be a marshal or a missionary?

But where did that leave the citizens of Moss Point? If he returned to the U.S. Marshal Service, it wouldn't convince Liz to coax a statement out of Charlie.

But if he stayed here on Spring Island, Charlie and Liz would be gone, forcing him to request another marshal with less experience dealing with children.

All would be lost.

Ian gritted his teeth. *So, God, why are You doing this to me?*

SEVEN

Liz was allowed to remove her personal things from the backseat of the car. They weren't much, as she had told the tow truck driver, and Ian could see now that she was right.

She really must have flown from the house, because all she had was her purse and a reusable shopping tote, printed with a picture of the planet and a grocery chain logo. In the bag were some basic toiletries and a few clothes, all dripping wet. Liz grimaced when she held it high.

"We'll take it to the rec center and let it dry in the ladies' room. No one is going to be using it in the next few days."

They walked back to the center, where Liz took a few minutes to lay out her things.

She reappeared a few minutes later and found him in the kitchen grabbing a cold glass of water. "Everything is soaking wet, but I think my ID and credit cards are fine. And I didn't have too much money."

"Good." Setting the glass down, Ian pivoted. "Liz, now that we confirmed what color of vehicle ran you off the road, it will help us in our search for William Smith."

"Do you think he's here?"

"There is no other reason for anyone to run you off the road, is there?"

"Elsie said Monica had borrowed money from some people who were anxious to get it back. Maybe they mistook me for her."

"Unlikely." He shook his head. "And I think it would be prudent not to get stuck on one hypo-thesis."

"So what are you saying?"

"I need you to press Charlie for a statement. I have shown him a picture of William Smith, but that was before he was talking. We need to show it to him again and ask him if Smith was the—"

"Forget it! I won't pressure him before he's ready. He is scared I'm going to leave him, like his father has. He's still trying to come to grips with that loss, and I won't add to his stress."

"He'll have you there to comfort him. Liz, we need to know."

"Charlie is scared, and like any boy, he's trying to push it away because he's not ready to deal with it."

Suddenly, she pulled in a hiccupping breath and blinked rapidly. "There must be some other proof that William Smith was there. Charlie may not have even seen a thing!"

"The police think otherwise."

"Well, they may be wrong. He just lost his father, and regardless of how I felt about that man, Charlie loved him. He needs someone he can trust. You don't fit that bill, but I do."

"How do you know that? You've known me for less than a day."

"You have a work schedule that is so full that you have time for one meal, and you've pawned Charlie off on the Wilsons."

Pawned Charlie off. Years ago, some relative of his had made the same comment. She hadn't wanted Ian and had asked why he was being pawned off on her. By that time, he was a troublesome teen with a heart hardened by all he'd had to endure after his parents' deaths. His extended family hadn't wanted what they considered the stigma of having a relative in foster care.

That was why he'd gravitated to Charlie. The same kind of childhood. Ian's mother and father hadn't been good at parenting. They'd been inconsistent, and his mother had struggled with alcohol and depression. His father had wandered in and out of their lives, until a DUI accident took both their lives.

Charlie's father had come and gone but without leaving anyone to care for the boy. His addiction was to cocaine and the search for a fast buck.

But even after all that, Liz's cool words cut deep into him. She was right. He was too busy to be any kind of guardian to Charlie. The marshals had felt that Charlie would respond to a male better than a female, but he had no time for the boy. He was a pastor now.

His unspoken words cut through him, right to his heart. He shut his eyes to the realization that he was just as much at fault as the relatives he hated.

And on top of that, he didn't like the selfish way he was thinking of Liz.

He hadn't sent Liz packing yesterday because she unwittingly became part of the WITSEC program. Charlie needed her, and Ian needed her to keep Charlie talking.

"All the more reason to get that statement out of Charlie, before things get a whole lot worse," he muttered, half at her words of pawning off and half at himself for knowing that he couldn't and shouldn't be looking after the boy.

"No." He looked at her and she went on, "I won't subject him to any more stress." She stared wide-eyed at him. "Do you have a car I can borrow?"

He couldn't lie to her. "I do, but because of the storm, I'll need it to evacuate the village."

"To move the people who don't have any other way off the island. I get it." She looked dejected. "What about this resort that's being built? Perhaps Charlie and I can get a ride out with someone there?"

He pulled a face. "If we got Charlie to identify his father's killer then we'd—"

"And if he's pressured, any good lawyer will get his testimony thrown out. As adults, we think that fingering the guy would probably help us grieve, but it's not so with children. It'll traumatize him further."

"So you think that the psychological damage will be worse than the physical damage? Think about how you'll feel if he's dead!"

Liz bit her lip, and as her eyes watered, he wanted to snatch back his words. But he couldn't. He had to be honest with her.

Yet the look on her face, the torn indecision, the worry and fear, made him want to stop the world and pull her into a hard embrace. Something that could block out all the bad stuff and let her think in safety. Let her see that as difficult as this decision was, Charlie's safety had to take precedence.

He gave into his compassion and hauled her close. And now, as he felt her grip him back, her hands locked around his waist and her nose pressed into his shirt, he found himself wondering which of their choices were better.

He didn't know, nor could he rely on his own painful experiences for the answer. The deaths of his parents, the distress of being plucked from one bad situation and shoved into another. To know first-hand how little a hurting kid was wanted. Maybe he was too emotionally attached here to make the right choices. But to call his supervisor and tell him that? Ian gritted his teeth.

He couldn't pull back his decision now. Smith needed to be caught. A cartel needed to be fingered and convicted. They needed to stop the horrible flow of drugs.

Still, his painful memories remained.

And he was only just beginning to admit how much he admired Liz for standing up for Charlie. He wished someone had done that for him twenty years ago.

Liz didn't know how she ended up in Ian's arms. Did he really pull her into a hug right in the middle of their argument? What on earth had prompted that? Still, she liked it. She *needed* it. She'd been running on empty, pushing herself.

But to end up wrapping herself around Ian, feeling his trim waist and strong arms and inhaling his clean, fresh scent…she, well, she needed the embrace.

And she felt as though Ian did, too. Something had driven him to become a marshal. Then to leave it all for the ministry? Her pastor had often spoken of the mistakes he'd made and lessons he'd learned. Ian seemed to have a tight grip on that part.

Like she had on him? *So why aren't you letting go? You like it. You're just like your sister, attracted to danger. Shame on you for not learning that lesson.*

Liz sucked in her breath. If she were to go on in the same manner, it would be as if her sister died in vain.

It was time to break this embrace. She peeled her arms from his torso and stepped back. Then she cleared her throat.

"Um," she began, looking everywhere but at him. "I still stand by my decision. We need to leave, and we need to give Charlie time to recover. Please don't ask again."

He rubbed his hand down his face. "I can't guarantee that, Liz. You know things can change at a moment's notice."

His words were calm, coaxing almost, in a strong kind of way. In another time, another place, she may have been interested in him. She might have considered his decisions more seriously.

But not right now. Charlie needed security and love. He needed a father figure, one who could be trusted to be home for him every night, but Ian wasn't that person.

And what did *she* want and need in a man? She wanted strength, all right, but this man, whether he wanted to admit it or not, was only too willing to be a marshal again. Did she want a man who was so relentless that he put the law above emotional well-being?

He took pride in his work, to the very limit. She should have a man who would love her more than his job.

Love? Good grief, she wasn't going that far, was she? They'd just met, just fought and shared a brief hug. Talk about jumping the gun on things.

"I know things can change quickly, but you can't rush grief. Haven't you ever lost someone you loved?"

He tightened his jaw. "I lost both my parents fairly young. When I read Charlie's file, I could see a bit of myself in him. That's why I agreed to take the case. So, yes, I've lost loved ones, too. I know all about grief, but—"

He stopped his words. Then he continued, "The cartel believes in retribution. They like to tidy up all the loose ends, and that will include Charlie. Even if he identifies William Smith and puts only him behind bars, they'll still want revenge. This isn't just about drugs and money. There are cartels fighting each other, and showing power is important."

A wad of bitter fear rose in her throat and ice seemed to grip her heart. Could there be someone out there besides Smith? Someone equally dangerous?

Her gaze skittered about the room, focusing anywhere but on Ian. She didn't want him to sense her fear and use it against her. "I have to go. I don't want Charlie to get worried about me."

Running away. That's what you're doing. Running away. You're scared you'll do the wrong thing and Charlie will get hurt. When your sister died, you failed to get him and take him away from that awful life.

She shoved away those thoughts. *Please, Lord, keep him safe. Give me the wisdom to know what to do.*

But as she slipped out of the center, into the heat unlike anything she'd ever experienced on the coast of Maine, she wondered if wisdom was so alien to her that she wouldn't recognize it when the good Lord gave it to her.

EIGHT

Liz closed the children's Bible she'd been reading. Both Charlie and Stephen had long since closed their eyes. The tiny window above the bed was open fully, and the gulf breeze had died to a mere breath, but that breath was cool compared to the heat of the day.

She gently covered the boys with the sheet one of them had kicked off sometime between David gathering the small stones and slaying the giant. Comforted by reading to Charlie, and smiling as Stephen's extroverted nature finally relented to sleep, Liz nevertheless finished the whole story.

Out in the living room, Elsie and George were talking to each other. They'd once again opened their home and their hearts to her, and she was grateful for the hospitality. Sneaking Charlie out during the night was no longer an option—even if she did have a car. Beside the fact that George was a bit of a night owl, it seemed wrong to pay back the couple's kindness with subterfuge.

She stood and stretched, not tired enough to crawl into the bed made up beside Charlie's in the tiny room. What she could do, however, was check out the village. If she needed to move fast with Charlie, she wanted to know the layout of the island, and be ready to leave.

Ready to leave? Liz's thoughts turned to the toiletries and personal items she'd left drying down in the rec center's ladies' room. She needed them.

Except Ian was probably down there, and she didn't want a confrontation with him again, especially after this afternoon. Their argument had ended in a tight embrace.

Quietly, she left the bedroom and padded down to the living room.

Liz fully expected to find George and Elsie still up, but in the living room sat only George, his soft snores in front of the TV telling her he'd fallen asleep. The sound of a shower told her Elsie was preparing for bed.

She'd wanted to thank the couple for taking in Charlie and to tell them she needed her toiletries, but it seemed unkind to wake up George.

Besides, they'd protest her going out, and yes, as much as she didn't want to run into Ian, she needed her things badly. She wouldn't be long, she told herself—probably back before George even woke up. Mounted on the wall beside the door was a rechargeable flashlight, and Liz carefully pried it free.

Then, quietly, Liz crept to the door and unlocked it during a loud commercial break.

Of course, the Wilsons would lock their doors, but Liz recalled what Charlie had said on the phone, something that had led her to find him here. But now it had a new meaning.

"It's small here, Auntie Liz. My new friend, Stephen, says the Everglades don't got cities. They only got keys, which don't make sense cuz no one used to lock their doors here, 'cept Monica. Stephen says now he's gotta make sure the door is locked all the time!"

Before, no one locked doors except Monica. It might have been because she's a young, single woman, but now another family locked their doors all the time? Had Charlie's arrival prompted extra vigilance? Or had something, or someone else, caused it? Like the man who'd run her off the road?

And Monica, what of her? Ian needed to confront her. He needed to find out why she'd been at his computer, printing out information on Charlie. Liz had heard Elsie tell Ian earlier that she hadn't seen the woman today at all. Perhaps Ian was doing something about her.

With great care, Liz padded down the steps and leaped over the crushed shell path to the sandy ground beyond.

The dirt road was impossible to see without the flashlight, and as she rounded the slight bend in the road, the security lights from the rec center came into full view. They had been hidden behind a house and a huge live oak that spread and drooped in the center of the village.

Under the tree lay a large dog, which lifted his head, barked once and watched her closely as she walked past.

The noise was deadened in the humid air. Now that she could see better, Liz shut off the flashlight and hurried toward the center.

Only one light was on inside. Ian was still working, his back to the window as he typed on his computer.

Someone had accessed Charlie's file. Was Ian searching now for proof of whom it could have been?

She should ask what he'd found so far, but breathing down his neck wouldn't help him find the answers any quicker.

And would it be a good idea to stick close to him after the rather intimate embrace she'd shared with him?

No. She should leave him alone. She'd only be in the way. And considering the heat rising in her cheeks at the memory of their embrace, she should let sleeping dogs lie.

Her decision left an odd feeling of disappointment in her, but it was too bad, she told herself. She had her own tasks.

She could take this time to check out the road to the causeway to see if the authorities had put up barricades. It would only take a minute.

The rec center's security light shone on to a dark opening near where that road entered the village. She'd seen the opening earlier today but not paid much attention to it. Not as wide as the road, it was still wide enough for an all-terrain vehicle, and she wondered if that was a trail to the resort, a shortcut, perhaps. In the quiet of the night, Liz caught a low growl, constant enough to catch her attention. Then it stopped suddenly with an odd, cough-like sound. It didn't sound like an animal. What could it be?

A short walk up the trail shouldn't hurt and might show her an option should she need to secret Charlie away. She'd been in the woods at the back of her house at night many times. She'd traipsed through dense, virgin forests at dusk. A trail here shouldn't pose any trouble.

Smacking a mosquito that landed on her neck, Liz picked up her pace. As soon as she entered the trail, leaves rustled ahead.

She focused her attention on the trail. It was wide, all right, and curved to the left, but enough of the rec center light filtered through the trees to guide her way. Careful where she stepped, Liz padded quietly around the bend and looked up.

Two men were talking, not twenty feet ahead of her.

NINE

LIZ could hear them talk, but the fast words were indistinct. One man, the taller one, whose back was slightly toward her, was the dominant one, throwing up his arms in what looked like frustration.

The smaller one, his head turning away and looking down, folded his arms.

In the dim light filtering through the trees, she could see little else. Who were they? Her heart leaped into her throat. What if they were here for Charlie?

Slowly, she began to back up, afraid to make even the slightest movement for fear of being spotted. Thankfully, though, both men looked deep in conversation. The bigger man shook his head and slapped a bug that landed on his leg, and in that instant, she caught a glimpse of his profile—strong nose, hawk-like, but broad, well-tanned and sporting a short goatee.

She even caught some snippets of the conversation.

"You heard me. Don't think I won't do it."

"All right! Just don't tell them, okay?"

"It's you who'll decide that, now, isn't it?"

They talked for a bit more, with Liz not seeing who was saying what. Both had deep voices. "The girl, too?" one of them muttered.

"I can't take…" A word Liz didn't catch. "…knows…you said…" Another jumble of words. "Just do it, or—"

"I know!"

She shivered and bit her lip. Something bothered her about the bigger man—the sinister nature he wore so easily as he towered over the other man.

Then, behind her, a door slammed. She turned her head slightly to listen more closely. She could hear a large dog bark and a man's voice tell it to be quiet.

Ian's voice. She'd noticed a dog lazing near the center when she'd walked down here and wondered if the animal belonged to him.

When she shifted her gaze back to the men, they were gone.

Immediately, cool air tickled her neck, and she fought the sudden urge to flee. The men may have noticed her and could be laying in ambush right now, waiting for her to move.

Slowly, she backed up around the bend, and when the trailhead came into view, she bolted.

* * *

Hearing a rustle, Ian looked up just as something entered his peripheral vision. Someone was coming toward him, fast, from the direction of the road and the adjacent trail.

Immediately, his hand reached for his gun, the movement sending his files and portfolio to the ground. After last night, he'd decided to carry his gun with him at all times. He'd also switched from his tucked-in button-up shirt, to a loose T-shirt that would cover the small holster attached to his strong side. It was important not to alarm the people he'd come to serve.

The figure stepped into the bright circle created by the center's lights. Liz? It *was* her. Relief washed through him as he shoved his gun back into its holster.

But what on earth was she doing on the trail at this time of night? He waited for her to approach.

The light above them highlighted her delicate features favorably. Wide eyes and smooth, pale skin that drew him into her, despite himself. Despite the fact he knew he shouldn't get involved with her. She wanted the exact opposite of what he wanted. Even if they'd shared a quiet moment in each other's arms, they were still worlds apart on how to deal with Charlie.

"Where were you?" he asked as she reached him.

"I came to get my toiletries."

He tightened his jaw. "They're not on the trail."

She looked distracted for a minute, then murmured, "I saw it and was curious as to where it went. Ian, there's—"

"The trail splits in a dozen different directions—" he cut her off "—one to a swamp, one to the springs here, some just meandering around. You could have been wandering around all night if you'd taken the wrong one."

Irritated, she shook her head. "This is an island, Ian. In theory, you can't get lost on an island."

"Even in the daytime, that forest looks the same in all directions. You can get lost and never leave a trail." He could feel his mouth tighten. Standing below the entrance light, he folded his arms and hoped his skepticism showed clearly, because, quite frankly, she had no idea of the dangers around her. "If you're thinking you may need to sneak away with Charlie, I would advise against it."

"It was nothing of the kind," she answered quickly.

Too quickly, he thought.

"Of course. Liz, if it was safe for you to take Charlie, I would insist you travel in the daylight, not by foot along some dark road that has no lighting whatsoever. In fact, there are no streetlights at all until you hit Northglade, and that's miles inland."

She bit her lip, and Ian knew the contrite look was genuine. Then, thoughtfully, she answered, "I'm sorry. And I had no idea about all those trails. I thought there'd be only one to the resort."

"The island is riddled with trails."

"You said springs? How many are there?"

"Two. The smaller one provides all the drinking water for the village via a pumping system. The larger one created a swamp and wasn't usable until Nelson Vincenti, the man building the resort at the north end, was able to control it. Now each forms its own stream system that drains to the gulf."

"I guess not too many islands around here have springs or else they'd be more populated."

Ian rubbed his forehead tiredly. He didn't feel like making small talk. "Most of the islands and keys around here are geographically unable to feature a spring, but Spring Island has a limestone base and the breaks in the aquifer have caused two small springs. It's atypical of the area, but we're glad for it, nonetheless."

"And the water is safe to drink?"

"With a small amount of treatment, yes, it's quite good." He glanced at his watch, which said it was well after 11:00 p.m. It was too late in the evening to be answering these kinds of questions. "You should get your things and go back to the Wilsons'."

Liz nodded. Her dark curls still bounced fresh-ly about her face, despite the long, hot day they'd experienced. She said nothing. Scooping up his paperwork at the same time as pulling out his key, he bit back another comment on her nocturnal wanderings.

Had she really just come to get her things, seen the trail opening and then decided to follow it, he wondered as he held open the door. It was plausible, and yet, she'd looked suspiciously guilty when he'd mentioned the possibility of her sneaking Charlie away. And she was quick to change the subject, too, he noticed.

She didn't trust him. A part of him could understand that, sure, but how was he supposed to do his job if she was sneaking around behind his back? He'd told her of the danger and yet, she seemed not to believe him. Frustration irked him as she brushed past him.

Even her mere presence affected him, despite the fact he'd told himself to forget her. She was nothing but a distraction, someone who wanted only to take Charlie away and forget about prosecuting his father's killer.

God, how am I supposed to do my work here with Liz making things difficult?

The answer didn't come, and he wondered if his distraction had more to do with her fresh beauty than her aim to keep her nephew safe at any cost.

He hated that he was either enamored by her looks or treating her as a fool. He wasn't the kind to waffle like this. Because he simply didn't know, he'd have to keep an even closer eye on her than he first realized.

On both Liz *and* Charlie. Great. Just when he didn't need the extra workload, either.

Poco, the dog who'd been barking a few moments ago, trotted up to the center. "Go home, Poco," he told the Callahan mutt sternly. Ian had convinced the Callahans to bring their children to Vacation Bible School, but the father, Leo, who'd recently secured work at the resort helping with the manual labor, had yet to agree to bring them to next Sunday's service. The small and wiry Leo was a quiet sort, though rarely home. He probably didn't realize how much of a nuisance Poco had become.

The dog stopped and then sniffed the air before trotting over to the trail. Ian watched the tan and brown mutt melt into the darkness.

"Let's get your stuff," he told Liz sternly. "Do you need a hand with your things?"

"No, thank you. I'll just shove them all into the bag. It should be dry, too."

As they stepped inside, barking started in the distance. Looking at Ian, Liz asked, "Is that the dog we just saw?"

"Yeah. Poco. He's the Callahans' mutt. He's never tied up. The only other dog here is an older couple's blind poodle. And he never leaves the house."

The barking increased, the animal reaching almost a frenzied state. The front door still ajar, Ian looked out into the dark evening. "He sounds upset," Liz commented. "He wasn't a moment ago."

"Yeah, it is odd." Ian frowned. The dog chased kids, rabbits and birds. He barked all the time but not like this.

The next yelp sounded like one of pain.

Liz grabbed him. "Something's wrong. Dogs don't go on like that without a reason. Maybe he's been bit by a snake?"

Ian had to agree. "Stay here for a second." He strode into his office and returned a moment later with a pair of night vision goggles. "Down the hall, last door on the right is a utility closet. The breakers are there. You'll see one by itself to the left that's marked Security Light. Shut it off, okay? It'll interfere with these night vision goggles."

Wetting her lips, Liz hurried down to the closet. Ian shut his eyes, giving them extra time to adjust to the dark. A second later, the light above him winked out. The only light inside the center came from the exit lights, but they wouldn't affect the goggles.

He could feel Liz return to his side as he lifted the goggles to his eyes. He searched the forest ahead, stepping out of the doorway and into the dark night to see better.

The brilliant green in his lenses told him where the heat was. He caught sight of Poco, loping back and forth, stopping occasionally to sniff the ground then bark and bay feverishly. Through the trees emanated a glow of something large, reflecting its heat downward. But it was too far to pinpoint accurately what it was. And without knowing how far it was, he couldn't guess the size.

Poco reappeared in his line of vision, this time closer, stopping again to bark and dance about.

"How do you see with them?"

"I can see a gray scale of whatever is there. Take a look."

She took the pair and peered in. "I see that dog and lots of trees. He keeps running back and forth and even deeper into the forest. Oh, he's gone now." She handed them back. "What do you think upset him?"

"I don't know. But it's too late to check it out now. We'll have to do it in the morning. At least he doesn't seem to be hurt. There's also a big mass of something hot to the right, but I don't know how deep in it is."

"Has the dog come back into view? You may be able to use its size to give you an idea."

"I can't see him." Ian lowered the binoculars. "Listen. He has quieted down. It must have been some wild animal getting him wound up."

Liz looked deep in thought. "What about that other thing you saw?"

"We'll check it out tomorrow morning. Whatever it was, it wasn't moving, so I don't think it was a threat."

She didn't answer. He looked at her concerned frown. "What is it?"

"I saw two men on that trail when I was on it. But they're not there now."

"Two men? Just now? Did they see you?"

"I don't think so. I was curious about the trail and walked just a little bit into it when I saw them. They weren't far ahead of me, but I don't think they saw me."

"It was dark. Are you sure of what you saw?"

"Absolutely. That light I just turned off went right through the trees to them."

"You didn't recognize them?"

She shook her head. "No."

"What were they doing?"

"Arguing, I think. When you slammed the door, they looked toward the rec center. I kept still, and I don't think they noticed me. Could they have been from the resort being built here?"

"Why would they be on the trail this late at night? Several of the men who live here work on the construction site right now. It could be that they were on their way home. They may have split shifts because of the heat."

"Maybe." She smacked an insect.

He waved away several bugs. "We should get your stuff and walk back to the Wilsons'."

Ian led Liz into the dark rec center. He grimaced as he realized that he'd left the door wide open. Every type of insect on the island could have come in. Quickly, he shut the door and hurried to turn on the lights, including the security light above the front door. Still holding her flashlight, Liz watched him, and when he lifted his brows at her in question, she looked away.

No. He wouldn't start wondering why she was looking at him. Not tonight, when he had other things to do.

"I'll just get my things," she said, hurrying into the ladies' room.

He needed to call his supervisor. There must be answers for some of the questions he had. Like how someone could beat Liz down here, assuming she'd been the target to run off the road and not some guy mistaking her for Monica. His boss was going to send someone up to her house to check it out. Maybe someone had broken into her home and found her flight bookings on her computer.

Ian glanced over to the ladies' room before he returned his night vision goggles to their case in his office. The set was expensive, and a recent update to the gear issued to the marshals. He was grateful for them.

Just as he closed the drawer of his filing cabinet, a scream tore through the center.

Followed by a loud thump.

Liz! Ian tore out of the office and spun left. He knew he shouldn't have left the rec center door wide open. If she was hurt—

If someone had snuck in behind their backs—

Yanking out his pistol, he reached the restroom in a few steps. He pushed hard on the restroom door, driving it against the wall. He tore past it before it could fly back at him.

"Ian! Look out!"

He stopped dead in the center of the restroom, his pistol at the ready. Liz knelt on the counter, her feet splayed out behind her and her fingers gripping the rim of the sink where it met the edge of the counter. Scattered all around her were her toiletries. She pointed downward.

Ian glanced down and leaped back. Beside the bag she'd dropped to the floor lay a snake—not just an ordinary one but a thick-bodied one about three feet in length and dark in color.

It was a water moccasin, its mouth open wide and ready to strike.

TEN

Liz watched in horror. She worked at a wildlife refuge and had developed a healthy respect for animal predators. She knew this one was exercising its predatory skills very well.

"Stay still, Ian! It's ready to strike."

Ian stood stock-still. "I can see that."

"And I'd say it's probably poisonous, too."

"Oh, yes. It's a water moccasin, like the tow truck driver was talking about."

Her stomach churned. "It must have come in with my stuff." She felt herself go weak and pale and gripped the counter to keep from fainting and toppling over at the thought she'd toted it back from the car. She should have shaken out the bag even after digging out the things that needed to dry. "To think, I could have been bitten…"

Ian took a small step backward, one barely noticeable. "Has it moved any?"

She shook her head. "No. I picked the bag up, and I was ready to put my things in but gave it a shake to open it. That's when the snake fell out."

Ian backed up another small step. Liz watched the snake intently. It didn't move. Apart from slithering a little bit when it fell to the floor, it hadn't moved at all. But its mouth gaped open, revealing a white interior as it tipped its head back. She looked up at Ian, who had taken yet another step back. Still the snake did not move. "See? It hasn't moved at all."

Ian frowned. "Something's wrong."

She let out a derisive snort. "Apart from the fact I had a huge poisonous snake in my bag? Whatever could it be?"

He ignored her biting sarcasm. He looked up from the snake. "I mean, that thing should be acting a lot more aggressively than it is."

"Really? All I noticed was a wide-open mouth and fangs. Then I jumped up here."

He quirked up a smile. "In one leap?"

"Yeah, no rebound board needed." She blew out a sigh. "But you're right. Something's wrong with it. It's not moving."

He reached behind him for the door and opened it gently. "I'll be back. Don't get down."

"Wasn't planning to."

He eased out of the restroom and ran into his office. In the key press, he found the key he was looking for and quickly hurried back to the storage closet. There, he found the tent bag, dumped it and grabbed the longest pole. After grabbing the ax from the rest of the camping gear, he returned to the restroom.

"What took you so long?"

"I needed these. Did it move?"

"No, thankfully."

He maneuvered the pole over the snake's head and lowered it down. The snake moved its head with odd slowness, as if drugged. But still it did not strike. The tongue flicked only once.

He looked up at her, his gaze calm, reassuring with a gentle hint of a smile as he nodded. "Ready?"

"For what?"

"Watch." As fast as he could, he slammed the pole down on the snake's neck and stepped on the length of graphite to pin the snake. It thrashed its tail briefly, but still, it didn't move.

Swinging the ax down, Ian cut off the snake's head. The harsh ring of metal hitting ceramic tile bounced around the quiet room.

Liz pointed to the bag nearby. "Okay, now shake that bag to make sure he didn't bring a friend."

With the pole, Ian lifted the mouth of the bag. "There's nothing in there."

She blew out a heavy sigh. She shifted her feet over the edge of the counter, then gingerly jumped down, feeling the ache of staying in an awkward position, especially after the bit of whiplash she thought she might have received from the car accident. "That tow truck driver was right to be concerned about snakes. Imagine it swimming into my bag." She shivered again.

Ian walked out and then returned with latex gloves and a large, clear plastic bag. He stooped to lift the snake's body by the tail. He avoided the head for the moment, knowing that it could still bite, even after decapitation. The body didn't readily lift up.

"It's stuck to the floor," he said.

"How is that possible?"

"I don't know. It must have stuck to your bag, too."

"I flapped the bag several times to open it. That must have loosened it. But why would it stick to things?"

Ian didn't answer her but rather examined the underbelly of the snake, tapping the scales experimentally. "There's glue on it."

"Glue? Whatever for?"

"I'm not an expert, but I think this snake was half dead when it fell to the floor."

"How is that possible? I mean, it would have had to swim into my bag." She thought again of how Ian had saved her from drowning. The sloppy, soft bottom of the inlet took its time absorbing her car, but shock and hitting her head on the steering wheel had caused her to lose consciousness, however briefly. She could have easily stayed underwater without Ian's help.

"No, water moccasins come out of the water a lot. That's why we have…" His voice faded. "Traps under the rec center!"

She peered at him, and after flicking the head of the snake into the plastic bag with the toe of his boot and tying the bag closed, he straightened. "I have to check something out. Let me use that flashlight you brought with you."

She handed it to him, then followed him out of the restroom and outside. He walked briskly around to the side facing the forest. He shone the light along the edge and stopped its beam halfway down. With the tent pole, he thrashed the thin layer of light-colored sand, sweeping the pole under the building slightly.

Then, on his knees, he peered under the building. A moment later, he reached in and pulled out a long board.

"What is it?"

"A homemade snake trap. It's just a simple device, really, but they can be very effective. You take a long board, smear a slow-drying contact cement on it and lay it down where you think the snakes will pass."

"They have mouse traps like that, too." Liz stared at the board. "Do you think this is where the snake came from?"

"Yes. See the mark it left? Even bits of scales. There was a snake here about the same size and thickness as the snake we have inside."

She stepped back furtively. "How could it have slithered in, then?"

"It didn't. Someone brought it in and put it into your bag. That's why the snake was nearly dead. It could have been here for some time."

She swallowed. "That guy who ran me off the road really wants me dead, doesn't he? He didn't drown me, so he's decided to poison me."

"Did you get a good look at the guy?"

"No. The windows were tinted, and the sun was in my eyes."

Ian slid the trap back into place. "Well, I don't think this was done by the same guy."

"How do you know?"

"Because I believe the guy who wants you dead is William Smith, and he really only wants to tie up his loose ends, like Charlie. He doesn't want Charlie to identify him. Running you off the road removed the chance that you would be taking him away."

"So what? He still could have done this."

"But how would he know about this trap? It's been here for a while." He set the trap back in place then stood and brushed his knees off. "No, I've read his profile. This doesn't feel like Smith's style."

She shrugged her shoulders. "So if you don't think it was him, who knows about these snake traps, and why would they want to kill me?"

"Everyone in the village knows about these traps. At our last community meeting, George suggested them because we didn't want the resort forcing these snakes out of their habitat and into ours. It's an old method of trapping them, and the old couple who owns the store helped set them."

She didn't know what to say. And she didn't feel like standing out here batting around ideas all evening. Her gaze wandered to the trailhead. She'd seen two men talking out there, and now, something niggled at her.

What was it? Who else would want to kill her? And why?

Ian touched her back, startling her. "Let's go. We shouldn't be out here. Let's get your stuff, and I'll walk you back to the Wilsons'."

They walked inside, Liz rubbing her arms all the way, feeling cold despite the sultry evening.

* * *

Ian studied Liz when she returned from gathering her things. He stood near the front door waiting for her, after she'd turned down his offer to come into the ladies' room with her.

Concern deepened her frown, and he saw her swallow. She was pretty, regardless of her expression, but she looked downright attractive right now, with her lips parted and moist from wetting them several times in the last few minutes.

Even though he'd set his personal life on hold while he helped Moss Point, she had an allure that made him want to protect her from all the ugliness in the world.

She blinked sky-blue eyes at him. "How does William Smith know where Charlie is?"

He sighed. "I've given that some thought. Perhaps by following you or tapping your phone line." Ian threw a glance at his office door. He'd locked it all up tight and shut everything off. What would he find if he went in there now? Or tomorrow morning? "I need to call my supervisor with an update. He may be able to tell us after he sends an agent to check out your house."

"I don't like the sound of that."

"Charlie told you that he'd thought you weren't coming because it took you so long to get here. Was your flight schedule done on the computer?"

"Yes. I printed it out for my neighbor. It took me all night to organize the flights alone, and it felt like forever getting down here. There were delays all down the eastern seaboard because of thunderstorms. I could have driven here sooner, but by the time I realized that we were landing in Fort Myers."

Lots of time for Smith to arrive. "Well, I'll learn more after your house is checked out. There could be information on your computer that would indicate you've had someone looking at it. Do you still have your house keys?"

"Yes. I'd had them in a zippered pocket in my toiletries bag. But it may be easier for the police to ask my neighbor. I gave her a key so she could take in my mail. I can call her and ask her to give it to them." She held up her bag dejectedly. "Of course, I'll have to use someone else's phone. Mine appears to have died."

"It's late. You can call from the Wilsons' first thing in the morning. And on that subject, let's not say anything right now about the snake, okay?"

"Fine by me. The sooner I forget it, the better I'll feel." Looking suddenly tired, Liz exhaled loudly. They had reached the Wilsons' house, and shortly after he saw her inside, he left.

The next morning, after grabbing a quick breakfast and calling his supervisor, Ian walked over to
the Wilsons'. He needed to tell Liz what he'd found
out about her house.

He stood in the doorway, watching Liz finish
washing the dishes. She turned and smiled a brief
greeting at him. But her eyes looked hollow. All
of the events of last night were weighing on her.
Heavily.

Charlie asked to throw toast crusts and crumbs
out to Joseph, who had stopped by. With the boys,
Liz walked out on the deck to watch them toss the
treats up in the air. Joseph perched high above them,
cocking his head at them in interest. In the distance,
they could hear Poco again.

At the sound of his dog barking, Stephen dropped
his crusts and galloped down the steps, calling the
dog's name. Ian walked up beside Liz on the deck
to watch Charlie continue his fun.

Charlie stopped throwing crusts. "Auntie Liz, Stephen says there's buried treasure on this island."

Liz offered her nephew an indulgent smile.
"Buried by pirates, I assume?"

"Nope. He says—"

A yell and a sharp bark interrupted his thoughts.
Ian turned to see Poco dance angrily around the
Callahan boy, his tail high and stiff, the hair on
his back standing up. Something lay at the animal's
feet. Something the dog refused to relinquish.

The boy reached down, but the dog defended its prize with a warning snap of sharp teeth. Stephen jumped back.

Liz walked to the edge of the steps. Poco turned and bit down on something long and black, then shook it with a wild thrash.

"It looks like a snake! This is awful! It's just like last night!" Liz cried, her voice tight as she started down the steps. "That boy shouldn't be so close!"

Ian pulled her back. Then after leaping off the deck, he tore over to where Stephen lingered. There, he yanked the boy away from the dog. "Get back, Stephen!"

The boy obeyed him, but Poco growled and bared his teeth. Ian spoke sharply to the mutt, who, recognizing his authority, dropped his prize and his tail before backing away.

It wasn't a snake he was defending, Ian noted as he picked it up. It wasn't even a meal.

It was a stretch of a narrow web belt, complete with gun holster. And smeared with something other than the dog's saliva.

Ian turned his palm upward, then looked at the defensive dog and the stains that had transferred to its scruffy beard.

The belt was soaked in blood.

ELEVEN

Liz took a hesitant step onto the crushed shell path. She could tell immediately by Ian's body language that something was seriously wrong. When Ian glanced her way, his face slack with shock and his hands smudged dark red, she trotted down the path to the dirt road. Ian stood at the far side, in front of the Callahan house and shaded by the spreading, moss-covered live oak.

The dog near him stood up and growled when she approached, but Ian yelled out, "Scram, Poco! Home!"

Head down and tail between its legs, the dog scampered a few feet away, then turned to watch the fate of its prize.

It wasn't a snake. For that, Liz was grateful, but whatever it was, it was leaving rust-colored smears on Ian's hands.

"What is it?" she asked. "What's on your hands?"

Ian looked around, forcing Liz to scan their surroundings as well. A young woman with a little girl hurried from a small house nestled deep under the far trees. Liz could hear George approaching behind her, and she turned in time to see a deep frown darkening his leathery features.

Beyond, several women and one man closed in. The whole village seemed to have heard the commotion and came to discover the cause. The man asked something, but she didn't catch it.

Ian spoke to the boy. "Go home, Stephen. Go wash your hands thoroughly, like we taught you in Vacation Bible School when we talked about the flu."

Confused, the boy retreated. Liz faced Ian as he examined the dog's prize. "It looks like some kind of military belt. But what's on it?"

"Blood, I'm afraid."

She gasped. "Are you sure?"

"It looks like it." He looked over his shoulder to George. "Can you get a plastic bag out of the container by my kitchen door? One of the big blue ones. The house is unlocked."

George nodded and hurried into Ian's tiny bungalow, only to return a moment later with the requested bag. He held it wide open while Ian dropped the belt into it. Blood smeared down the inside of the clear blue plastic.

"What are you going to do with it?" Liz asked.

"I'll put it into the freezer for the time being," Ian said, watching George tie the bag.

"Do you think it belongs to one of the villagers?"

"It's a military style web belt with half of a holster attachment, Liz. There's no one here who would need a handgun."

"A holster?" she echoed. "Maybe it belongs to one of the resort's security guards. Surely they would have someone on staff that's armed."

Ian shook his head. "Then why would it be soaked with blood?" He turned, and seeing the crowd forming, he spread out his hands. "Nothing left to see, folks. Go home. George and I will sort this out."

He turned to Stephen's mother. Remnants of the tape belonging to the police and fire department crisscrossed her house. She'd heard from Elsie that the police had been back with the fire marshal and taken away more things and asked more questions.

"Jenny, tie that dog up," Ian told the woman firmly. "If he's been into something he shouldn't have, he can't be allowed to wander the village."

Liz watched as Jenny Callahan grabbed the dog by its collar and led it around to the back of the house. Everyone else seemed to respect Ian's command and began to filter away.

Even Monica, Liz noticed as she allowed her curious gaze to drift throughout the village. She'd spied the woman coming down the road, in from the direction of the rec center. Today, she wore a different dress, a faded blue one with cap sleeves, similar in style to another dress Liz had been loaned. She caught Liz's stare and immediately turned away. Shock and fear showed clearly in the young woman's expression. Liz watched her bite her lip and wring her hands.

In the next instant, the woman spun back in the direction she'd come, hurrying past the rec center. She glanced over her shoulder at the thinning crowd, then at the small store and its owners. She disappeared into the forest at the trailhead.

Liz stood cemented to the dirt road, watching to see if Monica would exit the trail again.

She didn't. What was she up to?

Why hurry away? To find the rest of the belt? How would she know where it was?

Liz turned toward Ian as he and George were walking into his home, presumably to put the bag into the freezer. They weren't looking back. They didn't appear to notice Monica at all.

She looked over at the Wilsons' tiny home. Elsie was herding both boys into the house. She'd assumed that Liz would go with Ian, and she'd keep the boys safe until they returned. She'd wash Stephen's hands and probably use that order from Ian as an excuse to give both boys a good scrubbing down.

While Monica snuck away. To do what, in such a hurry?

If Liz called out to Ian, Monica might take off. And Liz was determined to ask her why she was so interested in Charlie.

Making a swift decision, Liz hurried down the dirt road, past several villagers as they dispersed. Breaking into a jog, she reached the trailhead seconds later. With a short glance at the quiet village behind her, she melted into it. That blood-smeared belt had scared Monica into action, and Liz was going to find out why. Because if it had something to do with Charlie, she needed to know.

It *had* to do with Charlie. A bloodied gun belt appearing after two attempts on her life? Liz refused to believe in coincidences.

The forest was blessedly cooler. It took a few seconds for her eyes to adjust. After that, she looked down at the ground. The trail was lined with hard-packed sand, like much of the island, and had been well used. It would be impossible to follow the woman's footprints.

Liz peered through the trees as she crept through the forest. She was really only about twenty seconds behind Monica. How hard would it be to lose her?

Ahead, something moved. Liz felt her heart leap into her throat as she spotted a flurry of light blue ahead and another darker blue deeper in. She dashed forward, fighting the natural rhythm of her awkward flip-flops, the ones she'd saved from the car. Not only were they noisy but running in them was nearly impossible. As soon as she returned to the Wilsons' trailer, she would change to her light-weight sneakers.

Ahead, the trail forked, forcing Liz to stop. She looked up the right fork, through the drooping cabbage palms with their spiky fronds. Which way—

There! In front of her was Monica, on her hands and knees, digging frantically in the soft sandy soil.

Liz gasped, and immediately Monica spun around. She was on her feet a second later.

"Why are you following me?"

Liz jumped back at the aggressive stance. "I saw you leave in a hurry. It looked like something was wrong, so I followed you."

"I'm fine. You should go back to the Wilson house." She brushed off her hands. The front of her dress was messed with sand. "Or better still, go home, wherever that is. You shouldn't be here."

"I beg to differ with you," Liz answered with a calm she didn't feel.

Taking a bold step forward, Monica tilted her head. Instantly, Liz could feel the woman's nervousness drenching the air between them even more than the humidity. Monica took another step forward.

Liz fought the urge to step back, to control her urge to flee. She'd learned years ago that she couldn't show fear. Animals, even the raptors that were her specialty, could sense fear and use it to their advantage.

"Are you really Charlie's aunt?" Monica barked out.

Hating herself in that instant, Liz took that step back. "Yes, his mother's younger sister. Why do you ask?"

"Where is she?"

"She died a few years ago." Liz felt her shoulder blades tighten together. Why was this woman so interested in Charlie?

"And Charlie's father?" Monica asked. "What happened to him?"

"He's also dead." She straightened. "Tell me, Monica, did Charlie speak to you before I came?"

The woman seemed surprised by the question, and she relaxed slightly. "Why, no. He didn't speak to anyone, not even Stephen. We all thought he was traumatized. That's what Ian said. He said we needed to be patient."

Liz wanted to tell her that he was none of Monica's business, so she may as well just forget about him. She wanted to take a few steps forward and show Monica she could be tough, too.

But such aggressiveness wasn't in her nature, regardless of how much she'd stood up to Ian.

Suddenly, she wanted him there beside her, as close as he'd been when he'd embraced her. "Charlie was doing what he thought was best and not saying too much. He's like that sometimes."

"I wonder who taught him that." Monica's expression turned hooded. "We all do what we think is best, don't we?"

The hairs on Liz's neck rose. Just how much did this woman know? Liz wondered. Was she the person who had accessed Charlie's file on Ian's computer?

Monica took a step closer, forcing Liz to lock her knees to stop herself from moving back again. "What do you think you can get out of him? Money? Welfare? That's not going to happen. We all need money!" She spat out that last word.

Liz swallowed a dry knot in her throat. She clenched her jaw to control the sudden surge of anger. There was no way ever that she would allow Monica near the boy.

No way ever. She opened her eyes. She drilled a hard stare at her. "Is there something you need to say? What's going on? Why are you so interested in Charlie? I know what you did with Ian's computer and I—"

Immediately, Monica lunged at her.

TWELVE

Ian shut the freezer door. He'd actually been thinking about donating this refrigerator to the Callahans. The bedroom that had burnt was right beside the kitchen, and the old refrigerator had shorted out in the fire.

But he doubted Jenny Callahan would want this thing after what he'd just shoved into it.

"This is the same kind of military web belt used in several Central American countries," he told George, who'd followed him inside.

"Are you sure?"

Ian began to wash his hands. "About four years ago, just before I left the marshals, I participated in Op Mac and Cheese with the Marines and the SEALs."

"Op Mac and Cheese?"

"A feel-good operation, created to foster the spirit of cooperation between various forces. To help overcome any feelings of distrust. We worked with some

Central American military forces, too. So we all could familiarize ourselves with how the others do things."

"And did it work? Do they get along now?"

Ian shrugged. "The jury's still out."

George chuckled. "Back to the problem at hand, how did a web belt used by a Central American country's military get on this island, and why is it soaked in blood?"

"We both know that this has something to do with Charlie."

Losing his smile, the older man nodded. Ian had filled in the ex-marshal with the details of how it was all tied to the illegal importation of drugs. Including how William Smith and Jerry Troop were implicated in an assassination attempt in Central America. Their cartel wanted a prominent politician killed. The politician was bringing the drug lords and crooked police officers to justice. He represented too much of a threat to the cartel, which had diversified into trafficking humans. They were losing the fear they'd instilled in the general population.

"Did Liz agree to ask Charlie about what he saw? I mean, he's talking to Elsie, but she ain't going to push him. She believes the boy will tell us when we've earned his trust."

"It may be too late by then," Ian muttered. "If William Smith is already here, we don't have much time."

George tapped the freezer door. "The guy who was wearing this thing may have already run out of time. There's a lot of blood on it."

Ian threw open his kitchen door. "Poco was hanging around the trail last night. But before that, when Liz showed up looking for her stuff, she saw the trail and followed it in for a bit. She saw two men talking there, but she didn't think they saw her."

"That may not mean anything. Besides, Poco's nuts. He chases Joseph around and barks at thin air. Maybe the belt belongs to the security firm the resort has hired. I wouldn't be surprised if you can buy belts like this one on the Internet."

"There's only one way to find out." He stepped outside and looked up. Though the sky was clear above him, the wind had increased and the humidity draped over him thick and hot and heavy. The back of his neck felt wet and sticky.

"That storm's building up steam, the forecasters say," George murmured, as if reading Ian's mind.

"Another thing to deal with."

"Look, Ian, you've got people willing to help you. Use them. You can't do it all by yourself. Call your supervisor, and let him know you need help. I know you also want to arrange for donations for the Callahans, but they're okay for the time being.

The fire marshal has cleared them to return to their house. The back end was added when their daughter was born and is still structurally sound."

Ian gritted his teeth. He was always busy but now more so with the weather and keeping an eye on Liz. Who could he ask to help? There were things only he could do.

He looked around. Speaking of Liz, where was she? She must have gone back into the Wilsons' house to help keep Stephen and Charlie busy. He needed to talk to her.

He'd called his supervisor this morning to ask about how Liz may have accidently passed information on Charlie's whereabouts. A special agent up there had discovered evidence of tampering with her phone line. A few screws undone and nicks in the paint proved a listening device has been added onto her outside wall. Most likely voice-activated, the man who'd investigated thought.

And though the agent had found several footprints in the soft soil, no fingerprints were found.

Ian shut and locked his kitchen door. He rarely locked his house here in this little village but knew it was time to start.

George had gone on ahead to his house and now was hurrying back toward him. Ian met him halfway. "What's wrong?"

"Liz isn't in our house. Elsie says she saw her walking toward the rec center, quickly, she thought."

Ian scanned the road in that direction. When he'd found the bloodied belt, he'd noticed Monica. Creeping up the road, their gazes had locked for a second, and Ian caught the guilt immediately. He'd already informed his supervisor, who was running a check on her. Ian had looked for her early this morning but hadn't found her.

He'd seen her hurry away, but he didn't want to drop the belt to chase her. Had Liz followed her? He strode to the rec center's front door and found it locked. Immediately, his gaze strayed to the trailhead.

He bolted over to it, noticing when he reached it the freshly broken branches, the small signs that it had been used recently.

Hadn't Liz come here last night? She'd denied planning to steal Charlie away but rather had claimed she'd been curious. Ian didn't buy that excuse at all.

He stooped to study a patch of white sand that had been scraped clear by a man's shoe. The print was too large to be either Liz's or Monica's.

Was it made by the man who owned the web belt? Ian studied the leaves, the sand, everything. There wasn't any blood around. And others used this trail, he admitted to himself. The village men whom Nelson Vincenti had hired walked to work this way because the trail was shorter than the road. Even Nelson could have walked here. He was a hands-on kind of man who preferred to inspect everything himself.

Ian straightened. He walked silently until he reached a fork. Again, there were signs of recent use but nothing he could recognize as belonging to Liz.

Something was wrong. He could feel it on an instinctive level that brought him back to his time as a marshal. Some days had been routine and boring, but some days had been anything but that. They'd spend days tracking a fugitive or hurrying a family to safety or busting down doors in the name of justice. The adrenaline surging within him had kept him going when fatigue would have easily won out.

Today was similar.

No. Different, he reminded himself. Liz was missing.

His heart turned cold in his chest. Where was she?

"Liz!" he called out. "Liz!"

All silent. Ian frantically scanned the woods, remembering what he'd said to her last night. The forests of the Everglades were devious. They were unique in every angle and yet, they were the same. Even he had to be careful and keep track of his route.

Still, he studied the forest floor. In this small hammock, pine and live oak shaded the ground, allowing air plants and ferns to flourish. Closer to the rec center, the forest was thinner, probably from decades of human use and exploitation. Here, this raised land was virgin and close.

Ian gasped. Through the thick branches and drooping moss, he saw something move slightly. Ian shoved back the branches to race up to it.

Liz! Relief swamped him as he dropped down to his knees.

She looked up at him, and he could see a red welt forming on her cheek. "Don't move. You may be hurt."

She shook her head. "I'm okay. Except this." She touched her cheek, then checked her fingers. "No blood."

"What happened to you? Were you following Monica?"

She looked up at him, dazed and blinking. "How did you know?"

"Because I noticed Monica walking away rather quickly, then you were gone, too, and Elsie saw you head this way."

She bit her lip. "I followed her. She took one look at that belt and ran off. You were…" She trailed off, then added, "She attacked me!"

Ian lifted her fingers to inspect her nails but found no defensive evidence, just damp sand. He hadn't been able to catch Monica yet. After this attack, though, he was going to make it a priority.

Ian pulled her back into his arms. She burst into tears. Eventually, her crying eased, and she hauled in a shuddering breath to calm herself further. He tightened his grip on her, rocking her lightly, wishing there was more he could do for her. He tipped his head down, his lips brushing her temple. He could kiss her, comfort—

No. He wouldn't risk losing his focus. He set her away from him. "Tell me everything that happened."

"I followed Monica after you took the belt into your house. But I…I found her digging." She stood and searched the ground in all directions. "I thought it was around here, but I don't know. After she attacked me, I fell. That's when she took off."

He stood, tipping back his hat. "Did she say anything to you? Tell you what she was digging for? Why was she upset with you?"

"Let me think." She worked her jaw, frowned and looked deep in thought. "I saw her expression when you picked up the belt. One look at it and she was horrified or scared or something. She turned and ran. I thought she might be up to no good and want to destroy some evidence, something left near where the dog found that web belt. And you were busy, so I had to leave right away or lose her. I didn't want her to destroy any evidence. You were already heading into your house…"

She cleared her throat. "But she did say odd things. What were they? She was talking about Charlie, and I asked her why she was so interested in him."

"Go on," he urged softly.

"Well, at first, I found her digging in the ground—with just her hands, no less. She got angry, asking why I wanted Charlie." She wet her lips.

Ian folded his arms. This behavior was totally the opposite of what he'd figured Monica to be. She'd been quiet and kind, saying little about herself except to explain that her immigrant parents had died a few years back and she was all alone. She started to craft souvenirs for tourists, she'd told him, but needed a steady job. He'd hired her to help with "The Shepherd's Smile."

Liz brushed back her hair and smoothed the light-weight dress he now recognized as another one of the set that Elsie had made for the women in the village. "She accused me of using Charlie to get money."

"I don't know why she said that. But taking off on your own when you don't know the area and attempts have been made on your life is foolish."

"I wanted to know what she was doing and if it was related to Charlie. His safety is my priority."

"And it's mine, too."

She tossed back a wayward curl. "Not completely. You want his father's murderer caught, that's all. So you can do your job with the marshal agency."

"Service. The U.S. Marshal Service."

She flicked up her hand. "Whatever it's called. That's your priority. But my priority is Charlie's well-being. Emotional and physical."

"We've been through all this, Liz. I won't rehash it. But think about what you've just done. I told you not to go onto these trails by yourself. And starting your own investigation was foolhardy. You say Charlie's emotional health is the most important thing to you, but you go off and put yourself in danger. How would Charlie react if he lost you, so soon after he lost his father?"

Liz swallowed. Then, with a furtive sweep of her hand, she wiped a fresh tear away from her cheek. "You're right. I shouldn't have gone off by myself. I wasn't thinking." After quickly biting her lip, she nodded and took a deep breath. "Thank you for reminding me of this. I do need to keep Charlie's well-being in mind." She straightened. "Yes, I need to keep that in focus."

Ian mentally shook his head. What had he just heard? Liz, the woman who'd corrected his mistakes, used logic and compassion at the same time, who was smart enough to locate her nephew, and refused to be made to feel guilty, was suddenly thanking him for pointing out a fault to her?

Whoa. He'd worked with a lot of ego in his time. Even in his days at college after he'd retired from the U.S. Marshal Service, he hadn't seen such honest contrition.

With the excuse of searching for where Monica had been digging, Ian looked away. He'd never been good at accepting criticism. Too many years of listening to how bad he could be, how difficult he was to control, each year worse than the last. He'd fought back and, even now, he hated when his faults were pointed out to him.

But Liz was showing a side of the faithful Christian few people saw.

Hear instruction, and be wise, and refuse it not, the Bible said.

Off the top of his head, he wasn't sure where that passage was found, but it didn't matter. It *was* wise to accept correction.

Guilt nibbled at him. Whether it was from his harsh words to Liz or because he wanted everything to be done right, he didn't know.

Forget it. There was too much to be concerned with.

"Since it's pointless to chase Monica now, we should get you to the clinic. That cut may become infected."

"A branch scratched me when I fell, but I don't think it broke the skin."

He reached out and touched her chin, moving her head to one side so he could study the welt. It really wasn't that bad, he decided. Maybe he just wanted her out of the forest, to somewhere safe.

"We need to search for whatever you saw with your night vision goggles," she said quietly. "It might have something to do with the web belt and Monica."

"But we *will* deal with Monica. For assaulting you and breaking into my computer." He dropped his hand and stepped back. "We'll need to backtrack a bit first. I memorized the angle from the center to help us find whatever it is more easily. Let's go."

They walked back toward the trailhead, but before reaching it, he turned and pointed. "It was in this direction." With that, he walked through the forest.

"You're bending to the left a bit," Liz noted.

He looked over his shoulder at her. "How do you know that?"

With raised brows, she looked deadpan serious and bluntly logical. "I work at a wildlife refuge. I've had to traipse through dense woods in Maine to follow injured birds. We only do that for the protected ones, but I've learned to go in straight lines without using a compass."

"How?"

"By picking one landmark in the direction you need to go and go straight to it. Then once you reach that landmark, you recheck your line and then choose another one. Landmarks can be big or small, just in the right direction. Weren't you ever a Boy Scout?"

"No. I wasn't really Boy Scout material." After a pause, he added, "You're right, though. I'd forgotten that simple rule. How far do I need to go to the right?"

"Only a couple of feet. Here." She walked to the right a bit and then pointed out the next point of reference, a bent tree with several ferns under it.

He nodded, and suddenly, she smiled at him. For that moment, he could forget about the welt, the contrition, everything but her smile. Her lovely, fresh smile that sucked the breath from him and tightened his chest.

At his waist, his cell phone vibrated and rang out its most basic chime. He pulled it free and answered with a short hello.

"Ian?" It was Elsie, her voice urgent and near tears. "You've got to come to the clinic! Charlie has been hurt!"

THIRTEEN

Liz knew something was wrong just by the look on Ian's face. He quickly hung up, and grabbing Liz, he ground out, "We've got to go. Elsie says Charlie's been hurt."

Liz gasped and ripped free of his grasp. "How? Where is he?"

"She says he's at the clinic."

"How far away are we?"

"Not far, really. We'll be there in a few minutes if we hurry." Ian pulled her through the woods, ignoring the trail as he crashed past trees and vines and ground his feet into the soft sand onto which everything seemed to be anchored.

Liz choked on her fear, feeling cold and hot at the same time. She shoved Ian's arm away and tore through the forest, cutting off corners of the erratic trail and slapping back large cabbage palm branches. Low growing vines were chewed up by her feet. Ian was right behind her.

Within two minutes, they broke free of the forest and found themselves to the west of the trail's entrance and near the back of the rec center.

A man stood outside, peering at the door. One of the men on the trail last night! Tearing past Ian, Liz ran up to him and grabbed his shirtfront. "You! What have you done to Charlie?"

Immediately, Ian yanked Liz away from the startled man. "Whoa, Liz, this is Leo Callahan, Stephen's father."

"What happened?" Liz asked, releasing him. "Where's Charlie?"

"In the clinic," the small, slim man answered, his expression one of shock. "He's not hurt badly, but he wants you."

Liz rushed past him, but as Ian began to follow, she heard Leo stop him. "You need to see this," the man told him.

She skidded to a stop and turned. Beside Ian, Leo stepped back away from the door. It lunged forward slightly, its top hinge broken off and its bottom one badly bent. The man grabbed it before it crashed to the dirt below.

Ian scanned the whole door and frame. "Someone broke into the rec center?"

"More than that as you'll see. The clinic and your office, too," Leo explained. "I found it like this on my way home for lunch. I heard Charlie crying and went inside. He was sitting on the floor, covered in blood."

Liz looked at the head of the Callahan family. The image roiled in her mind, and yet, with a frown, she recalled his words.

The man walked to his work at the resort early every day? And he had heard one small boy crying, at the back of the rec center?

She glanced at Ian, whose gaze dropped to the man's arms. Following it, she saw scrapes and scratches on him.

"How did you get those cuts? From this door?" Ian asked.

"No. We were securing the last of the solar panels recently before it got too hot, and one scraped along my arms when it shifted."

With a swift look around, he cleared his throat and lowered his voice. "I'd rather clean myself up than go to the first aid station. I don't want to miss any work time, especially if that storm hits and we all lose the work. I can't afford not to work. They gave me a day off to sort out my house, but I need the money to get it fixed. I don't got insurance, you know."

Liz turned away. Ian had this under control. She'd tell him later that Leo was one of the men on the trail last night. But first, she needed to see Charlie.

The clinic door was wide open, and inside Charlie sat on the exam table, the same one she'd rested on after her ordeal two days ago. Some bloodied gauzes lay on the tray set on a nearby table. The smell of antiseptic clung to the hot air. She felt her heart plummet, her stomach flip. She knew that scalp wounds bleed like crazy, but a child's, one in her own care, changed the rules of emotion drastically.

In front of Charlie stood Elsie, pressing a wet cloth to his forehead. "What happened?" Liz croaked out.

Elsie calmly removed the cloth, revealing a nasty gouge at his hairline. Liz approached, feeling the dread increase. Blood had been wiped from Charlie's face, but a few smears remained around the little boy's pug nose.

"Is he okay?"

"It's not so bad. We've just had a good scare. And we've already prayed about it."

"Thank you." She peered at Charlie, then sat up on the table to wrap her arms around him. "Leo says you were in here, crying. Why were you in here?"

Charlie looked down and shifted closer to Liz.

"He hasn't said a word." Elsie wiped her eyes with the back of her hand. "It's my fault, Liz. We were making a snack when Charlie said he saw that crazy bird, Joseph, and wanted to throw it some more crumbs. I let him. I shouldn't have, but the bird was sitting right on my deck again. He followed it here." She paused, as if wanting to add something but wasn't sure.

"It's all right, Elsie," Liz told her, reaching out to the woman with her free arm. "Look at the floor. There are some bird droppings in here. I think Joseph roosted in here a while. And the only way that could have happened is if this place had been broken into before Charlie left the house." She looked down at the boy clinging to her. "Is that what happened, sweetie? You can tell us."

Charlie, with eyes tightly shut, refused to answer.

Back to square one, except worse, now, she thought. The boy wouldn't even talk to *her*. Was this some kind of posttraumatic stress symptom? She took in the vandalized clinic. Besides the evidence that a large bird had roosted the night away in here, there were supplies scattered about.

Elsie moved forward. "When I found Charlie here, Leo had just arrived." She looked over her shoulder then back again. "Charlie must have cut himself on that cabinet door," Elsie said, finishing up with the bandage. "It swings outward fairly easily, and its corner is sharp." She sighed as she looked around at the mess. "It must have hit him when he was trying to catch Joseph."

"And then he cried for help," Liz finished. "Is that what happened, Charlie? Is that when Leo heard you?"

"Don't ask him leading questions, Liz," Ian said from the doorway. "Let him tell you first."

She scowled at Ian, but he carried on, "My office has been broken into, also. It doesn't look like anything is missing. But I can't say for sure until I do a thorough search."

"The clinic and the office," Leo muttered as he appeared beside Ian. "Probably kids vandalizing more than anything else."

"Maybe," Ian answered, looking over his shoulder. "But I can see the kitchen from here, and nothing is messed up there. The kitchen would have been a target for sure, if teens were involved. They know there's food and cold drinks there. But look, it's as neat as a pin."

"Not if they were in a hurry," Leo countered. Liz watched him. His cuts were cleaned up, but she could see that his nails were dirty. He may have washed his hands when he'd administered self first aid, but he hadn't cleaned under his fingernails. Even from this distance, she could see thick brown dirt under them.

Pulling together her bravery, Liz asked, "Leo, you were on the trail last night. Did you see anyone or anything around this center?"

Leo's face scrunched into a dark frown. "No one."

After shooting Liz a sharp glance, Ian asked, "What were you doing on the trail?"

"Coming home from work. Like I said, we're trying to get things secure before the storm. And the shifts are split now because of the heat."

That made sense, Liz thought. Hot countries all over the world took a break in the middle of the day. It can't be fun working in the early afternoon outside. Not in July, anyway.

Ian nodded before resuming his questions. "Leo," he began, "it's not quite lunch yet, but you said you were coming home for lunch. Did you take the trail or the road?"

Leo didn't look up. "The trail. I always take the trail. It cuts off at least fifteen minutes. You know that."

"You don't take your lunch with you?"

Leo hesitated. "Um, not always."

"Who was on the trail with you last night?" Ian asked. "Liz said there was another man there."

Leo threw her a scrutinizing look. Liz tipped her head down on the pretense of comforting Charlie. "It was Mr. Vincenti," the man answered.

The man who was building the resort. The man who was financing "The Shepherd's Smile." In one sense, he was Ian's boss, too. She glanced over at Ian to catch his reaction.

There wasn't any she could see. "Did he say why he was on the trail?" he asked.

Liz peeked up at Leo's expression. The man shrugged his shoulders. "He walked a bit with me when I was coming home. He didn't say why he was there, and it ain't my place to ask him."

"What did you talk about?"

"He talked about the village and the resort." Leo's mouth twisted, and Liz thought she saw his eyes roll slightly. "The guy wants as little impact on the environment as possible. He's hired you, he says, to help this village."

With his derisive words, the man shifted his eyes away. Elsie had mentioned Leo after the fire, saying that he wasn't a believer. Did Leo think that hiring Ian was a waste of money?

The gestures and body language she'd witnessed last night didn't quite mesh with Leo's report. Unless he was blasted and cut down a notch by the boss for some reason.

Behind the men, in the doorway, Leo's wife appeared. "What's wrong?" she asked no one in particular, taking in the whole scene with wide eyes.

"Charlie just bumped himself, that's all," Liz said, meeting the woman's shocked stare.

"We've had a break-in sometime in the night," Ian answered.

The woman swallowed and threw a fast glance at her husband.

"There, all done," Elsie said, patting Charlie's hand. "Does it hurt now?"

Charlie snuggled closer to Liz, prompting her to ask him the question herself and worry about what they'd say to Monica later. "Does it hurt, Charlie? Does any other place on you hurt?"

Tightening his lips, Charlie refused to answer. Liz bit her lip. This wasn't good. She didn't want to pressure Charlie into identifying who had killed his father, but she knew she'd have to pressure him to tell them where it might hurt.

Another thought struck her. If and when he did give a statement, a good lawyer might get wind of this latest refusal to speak and use it against those trying to bring Jerry's killer to justice.

No, don't leap ahead, she told herself. *One step at a time.*

"Liz?"

She looked up into Elsie's eyes as the woman spoke. "I'll take Charlie back home. And he won't be allowed to go outside this time." Elsie gave her a solemn shake of her head. "I shouldn't have let him out of my sight. I'm so sorry."

"I followed Joseph," Charlie's tiny voice whispered. "He flew in here."

Liz set him to her right and peered hard at him. Charlie looked nervously around at the group. Liz glanced up at Ian, noting, she was sure, his look of relief that the boy was still willing to talk.

"Joseph came in here, and I...hit my head on that door." Charlie pointed to the cabinet door. "Mr. Callahan found me and scared me, that's all."

"Why did he scare you?" Ian asked. "Was he in here, too?"

"He came in and closed the door. But Elsie came and got me." Charlie looked at Liz. "I shouldn't have chased Joseph. I'm good at doin' what I'm told, Auntie Liz. You're not going to leave me alone cuz I took off, are you?"

Liz looked over at Ian but found him swimming in her unshed tears. When she looked back at Charlie, she forced a smile onto her face. "I'm not going to leave you alone. But you misbehaved, and we'll discuss the punishment later, okay? You shouldn't go off without telling someone where you're going."

Charlie nodded. "But I had to when Dad was sleeping. He said I was allowed to."

She gave him a skeptical look. "Really?"

"Yes. I would take money and give it to friends of Dad's, even late at night. I could even spend his money, Dad said. Just not the big bills he kept in the globe you bought me. Only the little ones and the change, so I could go to McDonald's to eat. And

Dad said I wasn't allowed to talk to strangers, like you said, 'specially if they asked where I got the money."

Liz listened, dumbstruck. "Your father said that?"

Charlie nodded. "And I wouldn't talk to anyone 'cept the guy at the counter. He would give me extra ketchup that I could eat later. I wouldn't talk, just like you always told me to. But I won't run away again, Auntie Liz! It hurt this time."

It hurt her, too. She tightened her lips to stop a sob from slipping out. Her own words, the ones she'd hoped would protect Charlie, were used by Jerry to keep his illegal activities a secret.

"Come on, Charlie," Elsie said firmly, taking his hand and tugging him gently. He jumped to the floor. "We need to let these people deal with this mess." With a promising nod to Liz, she took the boy out of the clinic.

"Leo's gone," Ian commented. "So is Jen."

Liz peered out past the broken door. "Leo was lying about last night. I'm sure of it."

Ian stalked out of the clinic and began to study the door. His focus wasn't there, she could tell. He probably had a million things going through his mind. He had a village to minister to, a program to get off the ground and a storm coming.

"I heard Elsie say that she found Leo here with Charlie."

"So he may have broken in here?" She came up beside him. "We should call the police. As for Monica, we'll find her again. We'll talk to her about pushing me down and such. I don't think she's ready to take off."

Ian nodded absently. "I suppose so. I should call the resort. Part of the program that the Vincentis are offering includes emergency security."

She watched him work his jaw. "That isn't comforting you, is it?"

"No." He shook his head. "With a storm coming, threatening damage to the resort, and this kind of expensive vandalism, they may rescind funding."

"Would they do that after hiring you and making so many promises?"

"If the storm destroys too much, yes. If vandalism gets worse, they may, too. I know they're faithful Christians, but there has to be a breaking point. I just hope that this isn't it." He straightened as if shaking off his thoughts. "There's a list of the clinic's supplies in that desk. Why don't you start the inventory while I call the police and the resort? And when this is all over, we'll go back and continue our search, okay? Unless you want to find Monica?"

"No, we need to get the clinic in order. Monica isn't going anywhere. We'll find her later." She found the list of supplies that the nurse kept on hand and compared it to what was scattered about.

It appeared that there were a number of basic items missing. Gauze, bandages, antibiotics, painkillers, and some bottles of stuff she couldn't pronounce.

She could hear Ian talking on his phone out in the hall—first to the police, then the resort and finally an insurance company.

They finished securing the rec center, just as the security guard arrived. The police were on their way from Northglade, but it would be a while. There was nothing they could do except wait—something Ian wasn't that good at doing, she could see from his pacing.

After a few minutes of briefing the security guard, he said to her, "We have time to follow that trail again. Feel up to it?"

"Of course," she answered, surveying the door. "I want answers, too."

"After what happened to you there, with Monica, it's okay if you don't want to go back. In fact, if you want to charge Monica—"

"No. At least not yet. It was a scuffle, that's all. We were both upset, and I'd rather focus on Charlie. I won't fail him again. But we do need to talk to her. I want answers, and I think we'll get them faster if we promise we won't charge her."

"Charlie should be giving a statement, Liz. It's more important now, and it won't hurt him." He watched her expression cloud, then added, "You realize that by not allowing Charlie to be questioned and by telling him he shouldn't talk to strangers that you've done exactly what your brother-in-law wanted and what William Smith and the cartel would like."

She glared at him. "No, it's not like that!"

"Jerry told Charlie not to talk to strangers, too, and you reinforced that. We know his reasons were criminal, but Charlie doesn't know that. By reinforcing what Jerry said, you're making it progressively harder for Charlie to talk. And it will be easier for the defense to successfully throw out his testimony."

He was right. And worse, by preventing Charlie from talking, he could easily *never* tell what happened, stating that it was too traumatic. If Smith was allowed to go free, many people could be hurt with the drugs he continued to sell.

But Smith would never allow Charlie to live, Ian had said. Was it too late?

Dejected and worried, Liz followed Ian to the back door. They left the guard promising to call them as soon as the police arrived, and Ian then detoured through the kitchen, grabbing a couple of juice boxes and granola bars for them. As they ate them, they trekked back to where they were when Elsie called. There, Ian spotted the large mass he'd seen through his night vision goggles. "Look."

It was a car. Liz felt her heart leap into her throat. She pulled in a sharp breath as she grabbed Ian. "That's it! That's the car that ran me off the road."

FOURTEEN

Liz felt her mouth go suddenly dry. When they were back at the center, she'd taken the time to have a tall drink of water, but now, it felt as though she hadn't drank a drop of it.

Gingerly, she took a step closer, still clinging to Ian. She reached out her free hand and whispered, "I'm sure this is the car that ran me off the road."

As her hand closed in on the hood of the small SUV, Ian stretched out his to pull it back. "Let's not leave any fingerprints, okay?"

She drew back, nodding. Then, with Ian beside her, she walked slowly around it. Someone had rammed it nose first into the heavy brush. She could see the tracks it had made. The road, the one from the causeway to the village, could be seen ahead between the trees. Crushed ferns and other plants showed the tracks.

They stopped at the passenger door. "Wow, this was it, all right," Ian murmured.

Liz nodded. The whole side was scraped and dented. The passenger mirror dangled crookedly, with a spiderweb of cracks in its reflective surface. The blue paint of the vehicle had been scraped down to the shiny bare metal, and in spots, Liz could easily see the remnants of her rental's paint. Red scratches and flecks stained both mirror casing and side door.

Slowly, Ian walked around the whole vehicle, stopping at the driver's side door. He took out his phone and dialed. Thirty seconds later, he was reeling off the vehicle identification number, followed by the license plate number.

Liz tried to peer inside, but the windows were dark. Getting as close as she dared without touching it, she could finally see through the tinted windows. The interior resembled the car she'd driven into the water. Clean, impersonal, nothing out of the ordinary. "I bet this thing is a rental, too."

After covering his hand with his shirt, Ian tried the driver's door, but it was locked. He walked, trying the other doors, but they, too, were secure.

"So, whoever drove this vehicle in here may still be around." Liz stated the obvious. "We have four crimes, Ian. Running me off the road, setting fire to the Callahan house, breaking into the clinic, and me being attacked."

"Five, if you include the poisonous snake dumped into your bag."

"Other than the attacks on me, they all seem so random, so totally separate. But let's face it. They have to be related."

"It would seem like a pretty big coincidence if they weren't," he answered.

"Well, the guy who drove this isn't here. Let's see if we can't find out where he went."

Ian looked up at her. "More skills from your wildlife refuge?"

"We don't usually chase injured animals in the woods because we often allow nature to take its course. But occasionally we are told about injured, endangered animals that need to be found and cared for. A few years back, we were looking for an injured lynx. We found the animal, but it was hard to track him. I became really good at looking for tracks. And respecting injured predators."

With that, she began to search the ground. She pointed to one spot. "See, this is where several people stood, besides us, that is. You can see two different sized prints in the crushed ferns. Both hard boots, I'd say. It's funny that closer to the rec center there is more sand."

"The village has been around for decades. George says his father helped build the original houses here. They were all fishermen back then. It was their wives who grew vegetables and fruit and who cut down the trees around the village for firewood. So it's been cleaned out and built up over the years."

Nodding, Liz kept her attention to the ground. "They went this way. They—" She stopped.

"What is it?"

Liz stooped as Ian came close. She pointed out to him what she'd seen when he bent down on one knee and shoved his hat up farther. "Do you think that might be blood?"

Ian studied the large brown smear on the cabbage palm leaf. He pointed to the splatters on the vines at the edge of the impromptu trail. Most of the blood had already been ground into ferns and air plants, but it wasn't hard to follow the blood, thanks to the bright green of the leaves.

"We have to follow this." Liz stated the obvious, but the danger they could be facing didn't escape her. Someone had lost a lot of blood. The web belt dragged in by the dog suggested that. And the amount on the belt had to be enough of a loss to kill a person.

This had something to do with Charlie, she just knew it. So maybe finding whoever was hurt wasn't the wisest idea even if he had a gun. William Smith wanted Charlie dead.

She couldn't leave a person to die out here, though, could she?

She swallowed. *Lord, take care of us. Help us do the right thing.*

No, she wouldn't ignore the fact that someone was hurt, even if it was Jerry's killer. They needed

to find him, even half dead, so Charlie could recognize him and have the police arrest him. They
needed to end this nightmare.

She stood, aching and drooping in the heat, feeling sweat trickle down her temples. Humidity made
her legs feel thick and heavy. Maybe she should
have asked Charlie to try really hard to tell them
what he saw.

Lord, give me wisdom.

The sun that had shone brightly had now slipped
behind a long, gray cloud. Through the canopy of
blowing trees, she could see the day was deteriorating. "It's getting cloudy out."

"And I think the wind has risen," Ian finished for
her.

"When was the last time you checked the
forecast?"

"Not since this morning. The FEMA people
have my cell phone, and so do the police. They
would have called by now if we were being told to
evacuate."

She wanted to ask for the details of an evacuation.
Where would the people go? How long would they
be away? What kind of security would there be?
Would they take Monica, even after she'd attacked
her? But right now, the trail kept her attention. She
pointed to two distinct marks along its edge. And

up a way, she found where blood had beaded on the dry sand. She followed it, hoping that she was doing the right thing.

"Look."

She followed Ian's hand as he bent down and pointed to the ground. A single line dug into the thin soil. As she followed it along one section where rocks and sand met, the line looked like divots spelling out some kind of Morse code signal. Short dots, a few long dashes, then a dot or two again.

Liz opened her mouth to ask Ian if he noticed that but stopped. Worry creased his brow as he stared up at the darkening clouds. She bet he was kicking himself for not checking the forecast more recently. If the tropical storm was heading this way and determined to become a hurricane, he needed to coordinate a possible evacuation.

These were his parishioners. They were his responsibility. He cared for them. Even if the storm missed them, everyone needed to be prepared. Up in Maine, they needed to be prepared for storms, though theirs were mostly in the dead of winter. Where she lived on the coast, the cold was tempered by the Gulf of Maine—cool summers and damp, cold winters.

She touched his arm. "It's okay. We'll find out where this trail leads, then we'll go back to your office and you can check on the storm. No news is good news, right?"

He nodded. "Yeah, you're right. It's just that this is my job, Liz. I'm supposed to take care of these people *and* take care of Charlie, and it looks like it's all falling apart."

"Sometimes that happens. My father died of a heart attack, and the next week, my sister died. I thought everything was falling apart. The week after, Jerry took off with Charlie, and I thought this is it. There's nothing bad left to happen."

"But Jerry came back."

"Yes. He needed money and knew I'd give him some in return for seeing Charlie regularly. I'd been saving my money for a good lawyer to try to get custody of Charlie. Instead, I gave most of it to Jerry. He promised to let me see Charlie, and I'd be risking a lot trying for custody. So I took his offer. I guess I'm not much of a gambler."

She sighed as they continued along the trail. "But you know what? I don't regret it. I'd been given an opportunity to bond with Charlie and have him know and trust me. If I'd saved the money, Jerry may have left the state and I may never have seen Charlie again." She smiled at Ian. "What I'm saying is that sometimes it doesn't look right or feel right, but it works out all right. I like to think that it's because I trust God. And I know He'll take care of me because I want His will to be first and foremost in my life."

He had been listening to her. She'd noticed his tiny reactions to her words. The slight tightening of the jaw, the way he blinked.

And he watched her still, even after she'd fallen silent. She felt her mouth twist up into a slight smile. When she was rewarded with a smile in return, her own fell away. Ian had a beautiful smile, so confident and full of depth and rich with a gentleness that reached into his eyes, across to hers and deep down into her soul.

Her breath left her. She was crazy to be allowing a smile to have this effect on her. Ian was devoted to this island, to his work, to his life here, to his marshal assignment.

And she needed to get Charlie away from here, to let him heal, to allow him to tell her what he'd seen in his own time, all the while keeping him out of harm's way, away from all the evil that may have followed her here.

There was no way they could reconcile the two needs, even if they wanted to. Ian lived to excel at his job and nothing else. She refused to be like her sister and believe she could change him.

Still, his smile mesmerized her. She found herself taking a short step closer to him and touching his face with her fingertips. His jawline was rough with a light-colored beard that he must not have shaved off this morning. He usually wore a hat, tipped forward to shield his eyes, but right now, it was shoved back, offering her a full view of his light blue eyes. She fingered his sideburn, lightly, stroking downward with the direction of growth.

His eyes closed, his mouth moved briefly. Was he praying? She had yet to hear him pray but surely as the village pastor, he'd pray often, wouldn't he?

If only they could find some common ground with Charlie. He wanted only one thing. To him, identifying Smith was too important to allow any other solution. But she could never allow it to happen. Charlie's emotional health balanced on a thin beam right now. Seeing him today pull away from people just because he'd hurt himself was proof that he could easily pull away permanently.

A screech sliced the air, and Ian's eyes flew open. Joseph, a wild brushstroke of rainbow colors, swooped by.

She and Ian ducked. The bird was acting almost aggressively. No wonder Elsie didn't like the crazy creature.

With that, she stepped away from Ian and all the temptation she'd felt with his smile. As nice as it would have been to feel his arms around her again, she couldn't allow it to cloud why she was here.

"Let's follow that trail again, shall we? I think the beach is ahead," she suggested quietly.

Indeed, the marks they'd been following led to the beach. They stepped from the dense growth onto a narrow swath of white sand. Automatically, they both looked up at the sky. Bands of gray clouds lingered far off to the west, while vertical columns of rain, made into a strong slant by the hard wind, connected the clouds to the heavy seas.

The ever-present wind had picked up, too, drawing choppy waters in to slap the shore.

"That way to the village, right?" she asked, pointing southward to her left.

"Yes. There's a dock at the end of the path between my house and the Wilsons'. No beach to speak of. Lots of mangroves growing right out of the water. But just over that small knoll is the stream. It's the runoff from the spring that services Moss Point."

The knoll wasn't far, but Liz looked down at the sand. The trail they'd been following led into the water, but the surf had washed much of it away. There was no blood on the beach, either. So what had been dragged here?

Not knowing what to do, she began to walk south and within a few steps spied the knoll. Liz turned left to peer upstream and into the forest. Fresh water had dug out a deep gorge on its trip to the beach and now lush ferns grew along the bank, securing the sandy soil from erosion.

She turned to face the water, and climbed up the small knoll to peer out at the waves.

"What's that over there?" she asked, pointing toward a shallow sandbank that was rapidly disappearing with the incoming tide. Ian looked down where the salt water lapped at the mouth of the creek. Water had accumulated in an open bowl that the tides had reformed into a small tidal pool.

The surf, increased from the impending storm, had shoved something against the inward side of the tidal pool. Ian waded into the warm water. "It's a hat, that's all. Kind of like mine."

"No, not that, Ian!" Liz's voice rose as she took several steps closer to him. "Over the knoll in the water."

Ian climbed up on the knoll and searched the shallow water. One hard wave caught the thing and shoved it on the shore. Liz saw Ian jump back.

Liz climbed up beside him for a better look. Then gasped.

Slapping against the surf side of the sand bowl was the body of a man.

FIFTEEN

Liz retreated into the forest. When she'd finished reacting to what she'd seen, and had splashed her face and head with the spring runoff water, she returned. She'd never seen a dead body before—animals' bodies, yes, but a person's, a human, no. Not ever.

Ian was on his cell phone, talking as he stood beside the body he'd flipped over and dragged up onto the shore.

"I don't think he's been in the water for very long. I had to pull him in or else the tide would have turned and dragged him out." He paused, listening. "Yes, it belongs to him. I can see the blood spatter everywhere but where the belt was."

Again, he listened. "Oh, yeah, I'd say he's been murdered. Stabbed and strangled, from what I can tell. Some fish have started to nibble on him. He's missing a finger."

Ian looked up as Liz approached. His grim, anxious stare locked with hers, but she thought for a moment that he looked like a little boy lost, like someone who needed her to hold him as tightly as she'd like him to hold her. Then he turned away and finished talking. "Call me as soon as you can get someone down here."

Closing his phone, he led Liz away from the water's edge. She knew she looked a sight, with her pale face and the wind thrashing about her mess of damp hair, but she hoped he'd see past her state for the moment.

And just hold her. Only for a minute. That's all she wanted.

He slipped his phone back into his pocket and walked over to her. Without speaking, he pulled her into his arms and held her tightly.

They stood as close as two people could get, Liz resting her cheek on his warm shirt, feeling his right hand plunge into her hair. She'd planned to cut it short this month, but with the cool, wet summer they'd experienced up north, it hadn't happened yet. Now it was thick with curls and sticking up all over the place.

"I'm sorry you had to see this," he said quietly, still keeping her a good distance from the man. "Especially after all that's happened to you."

It felt so good to hold him. She could sense his strength, and somehow, it seemed to seep into her. She lifted her head, wanting to smile, but it didn't come.

Instead, she parted her lips to speak, to say thank you for all he'd done for her and Charlie, but the words didn't come, either.

Just as well. Ian dipped his head and touched her lips with his. A light kiss, barely above the slightest brushing of lips, a kiss that trailed over her cheek and swept upward like a feather, but it warmed her more than the oppressive heat and humidity could ever.

She wanted to hold him together until all the pain and fear drained away.

But now wasn't the time for this.

She stepped out of his embrace, feeling embarrassed at the crazy yearnings that were popping up at the most inappropriate moments. Ian was so much better at this—well-trained, strong in the face of death, while she was a mess.

A thought hit her. She expected to be able to take care of Charlie when she couldn't handle this?

No, *this* was too much for any regular citizen. She shouldn't be so hard on herself.

But still, the little thought had already done its damage. Thankfully, they were far away from the dead man.

But she'd recognized the man from her first glimpse. He'd been the one talking to Leo the night before. And yes, she remembered the clothing. This man was—she recalled the name Leo had mentioned—Nelson Vincenti.

"At least we know who was wearing the belt that Poco found," Ian said.

"Are you sure?"

Concentrating, she tried to recall if this man had worn a web belt last night. Was he? She remembered the short sleeved shirt, the light khaki pants with the pockets on the sides of the thighs. The shirt had been tucked in…

Yes, there had been a belt. Not a wide one and not a light-colored one, either. Yes, he'd been wearing a belt that matched the one Poco had found.

Automatically, she glanced around. The shoreline here was narrow, the only decent sandy spot being where the creek fed into the gulf. Beyond that, the trees, those crazy alder-like trees that grew out of the water, along with spiky palms and scraggly, twisted pines.

She peered into the forest as much as it let her but saw no one. "Who could have done this?" she whispered, half to herself.

"Unless there were two people involved in finding Charlie, I don't know."

"What do you mean, two people?"

"Sometimes a cartel or syndicate will send another person after the first assassin. That person is to kill the first if he is unsuccessful."

She shook her head. "Why would Nelson Vincenti be involved with organized crime? You said he was a Christian and had started 'The Shepherd's Smile.'"

Ian's expression was almost laughable, if she actually felt like smiling. He slowly shook his head. "You think this is Nelson Vincenti? Why do you say that?"

"Because Leo said so. This is the guy that was talking to him last night on the trail."

"Are you sure?"

"Absolutely. I recognize the clothing, and I saw the man's profile. That big nose."

She watched Ian peer at the man. He was laying chest down, but his face was turned toward the surf. As horrible as the sight was, she knew what she saw. A large, hawk-like nose. "Yes, I'm positive this is the man Leo was talking to. And he said the man was Nelson Vincenti."

"No, Liz," he answered quietly. "This is William Smith. I've met Nelson on several occasions, and I have several photos of Smith. *This* is Smith." He paused, then dug out his phone. "And I can prove it to you."

He played with a few buttons for a minute, then showed her the phone picture he'd pulled up. "This is William Smith. It was taken two months ago in Guatemala City, by a mole the U.S. government has down there. Our government wants to keep a certain politician in power because he's successfully fighting the cartels. Jerry Troop and William Smith were implicated in an attempt on the guy's life—a test of loyalty for Jerry."

Liz took the phone. Its screen showed the man at their feet, sitting at an outdoor café, his face in full profile. He held a small white cup in his hand, and his companion's arm was easily seen. It was a man's skinny arm, with a tattoo similar to Jerry's.

She swallowed. Last night, she'd been so close to Smith that if she'd moved even slightly her position would have been revealed. What would he have done, then? Shot her where she stood? The thought churned in her stomach.

She handed back the phone. "Leo lied to us?"

"It would appear so, but we have to consider another theory. That Leo was lied to, himself."

"How could that be?"

"It's unlikely that Leo would know the resort owner, much less carry on a conversation with him in the forest. He'd have been hired by an HR person on-site or even by the contractor or his personnel. And Smith was bold enough to try a lot of things. He once impersonated his cartel boss, Mario-Josef Sabby, and brokered a deal between Sabby and a British crime boss. Sabby put a contract out on Smith for that but rescinded it later, when the deal worked in his favor."

"So it's possible Smith lied to Leo. What did you say about a cartel sending another person after the first? To kill the first if he is unsuccessful?"

"That's the way it works sometimes. But not here, I don't think. Like I said before, this has a personal feel to it, like someone was mad at this man, rather than a necessary assassination. Besides, it's only been two days. As much as Charlie has snuck out of the house, Smith couldn't have been watching the place every minute of the day. He would have to be patient. At least to a degree. And we don't know when he got here."

"And you altered Charlie's appearance. It's possible that he isn't sure which boy in the village is him." She shivered. "That must have put the others at risk. Stephen is closest in size to Charlie. Ian, all the boys in the village could be at risk!"

Ian nodded. She knew her words had a heavy impact on him, but still, it was scary to think that Smith might have considered killing all the boys to get what he wanted. She felt sick just thinking about it.

"So you think that the person who killed him wasn't someone who thought Smith had failed in his mission?"

"That's just an initial reaction. We can't say for sure."

She glanced briefly at the body, then turned away. "He must have been the one who tried to run me off the road." She blinked at Ian. "But how did he find me? How did he get down here so quickly?"

"Your phone line had been tapped."

"Do they know for sure that Smith did it?" Just the thought of having Smith so close to her. He'd followed her home, for sure…

She gasped.

"What is it?"

Biting both her lips, Liz peered down at the man, trying to see past the idea of a violent death. She tried to see the man as being alive. The hair was the same, the popular beard style. "When I saw this man last night, he gave me the creeps. I thought it was just because the whole thing felt sinister, but no, it wasn't that. I think I've seen this man before."

"When?"

She swallowed and gave a hasty shake of her head. "Last Sunday, after they told me Charlie had been killed. Once I got home, I called my pastor and walked into the village. I met him at the church and we talked for a bit."

Pointing down, she continued, "I remember walking back and seeing this man in a car, driving on the road away from my house." She furrowed her eyebrows. "The road goes down to the water, so I didn't think anything of it at the time—just that it was a stranger. You see, we don't get too many of them, even in the summer. The people who can afford boats tend to hang out at coastal villages with good water access. We just have a few rickety stairs going down to the rocks."

"It's possible that he hooked up the listening device then. That means he knew who you were and where you lived *and* guessed that Charlie had been taken into custody and you might hear from him."

"That seems like a lot to assume." She grimaced. "Maybe he thought I had him."

"Not really. He may have known about you for some time before he killed Jerry. Even known where you lived, especially since you had contact with Charlie and Jerry. Is your house secluded?"

"Very much. I have trees on all sides, and my neighbors aren't close. I brought Charlie there once, and he really enjoyed the woods." She looked up at Ian. "Was your agent able to find any fingerprints?"

"None. It's obvious Smith wore gloves or wiped everything down."

She cringed at the thought of Smith coming to her house.

The wind picked up then and buffeted Liz. She didn't want to be out on the beach anymore. She should be feeling better now that Smith was out of the way, no longer a threat to Charlie, but comfort didn't come. Someone had murdered this man.

"What now?" she asked Ian, surprised to find him looking at her closely.

"I've called my supervisor and the police. We shouldn't leave the body here. We're due to get a storm surge."

"How bad will that be?"

"Historically, they've always predicted higher than what actually comes. The last big hurricane to hit had a much smaller surge than expected. But on this island, a storm surge of just a few feet could do a lot of damage. We're right at sea level, unlike the resort, which is on a slight elevation."

"The police will come soon, won't they?"

"Yes, but some evidence may still wash away. Something we could be missing. I haven't worked a crime scene before. My job was to take the witnesses and deal with them." He flipped open his phone. "We'll need to secure this area, and the resort can help with that."

"Maybe you can ask them about Leo? Such as, has he ever met Nelson?"

Ian nodded. "Good idea." He called the resort and talked briefly with them. Then he hung up. "They're coming."

Liz knew that they had to stay here until someone came but shivered at the thought. Then, she walked over the knoll and sat on an ancient log. The sound of water gurgling, barely heard over the wind and pounding surf, comforted her.

She watched Ian. Methodically, he searched the shoreline around the body—slowly, in great detail.

He was good at being a marshal. And despite the grim circumstances, she knew he appreciated doing that work.

Her thoughts returned to why they were here. Smith was dead. And because of that, Ian could give up his job as Charlie's protector. Soon, Liz knew she'd get the chance to take the boy home. She'd love him, care for him and be the mother she'd wanted to be to him after her sister had died.

She'd leave soon. A short, hard pang of yearning hit her, and she swallowed down the lump it caused. Because she would soon leave Ian? Because Charlie might miss him?

That couldn't be helped, she told herself sharply. Ian belonged here. He would give this town his all, and any personal relationships would have to take a backseat. What woman in her right mind would want that kind of relationship?

She knew she must take Charlie away, to start a new life that wouldn't remind him of all he'd lost. After her father had died, her mother had moved the family out of the home that they'd all shared for fifteen years because the house reminded her too much of Dad.

Liz couldn't allow Charlie to stay here.

She cast a long look at Ian, his slim form bent down to look at something in the sand. His expression was full of concern and concentration.

Again, regret hit her hard.

SIXTEEN

Ian was glad when security arrived from the resort. When Nelson had first offered to assist the village should they need some of the services being set in place, Ian had expected only firefighting and the occasional medical service would be used.

He hadn't thought he'd need security to not only guard the rec center but also to babysit the remains of a killer.

The security chief arrived shortly after two of his men. Ian had met the man once and had checked out the company and the man the next day. They both came highly recommended.

Ian approached him. "I'd like to ask you a few questions, if you don't mind. Just about one of your employees. His name is Leo Callahan."

"Sure," the chief said. "Do you think he's involved in this murder?"

"I don't know. You recently hired him from the village?"

"Not me, but HR did. I did a basic background check on him, that's all."

"What did you find?"

"Nothing unusual, no convictions," the big Hispanic man said with a shrug. "He wanted work because he needed the money, like everyone else. He said his last job was on board a charter boat up near St. Petersburg, but he was laid off when the economy collapsed. He helped paying passengers fish for amberjack and king mackerel. The passengers got to keep the fish after the crew dressed and wrapped them."

Ian reacted to the chief's words. So Leo would likely own a good filet knife. Mind you, Ian added to himself grimly, he probably had one in his own cutlery drawer. He'd been given the house after one of the longtime residents passed away and Annette Vincenti had bought it for "The Shepherd's Smile" pastor.

Still, Leo would be comfortable using a filet knife, whereas Ian had never dressed a fresh fish. He twisted his mouth. Not a strong lead by any means. And it still didn't discount Monica and her strange behavior.

"Has anything really unusual happened at the resort lately?" Ian asked.

"I've worked a lot of construction sites but, except for this here—" he pointed to Smith "—this site is fairly normal. Oh, we've had a few thefts here. First up, we had our petty cash stolen. It wasn't much—a few thousand dollars."

"That's a big petty cash."

The chief nodded. "We don't get into the city often, and sometimes we need a worker for only a day or two. A temporary wage, plus other daily incidentals, can eat up a petty cash fund fairly quickly. The money was in a locked box, out of the safe for just a minute or two, and then it was gone."

"Do you suspect anyone?"

"No one. The secretary who was responsible for it is extremely upset and has been with Mr. Vincenti for years. She was our most likely suspect, but I don't think she did it."

"You said there were other thefts?"

"Small stuff. A lunch here and there, and one worker lost his spare pants." The chief shook his head. "We've been kept busy with the storm coming. The site manager has been told to prepare for possible evacuation, so we've been securing everything. We even moved the barricades away from the causeway in case we need to move the heavy equipment."

That explained one mystery. "It's risky work, building a resort in a hurricane-prone area," Ian commented, fishing for a reaction.

The chief looked blasé. "The whole Gulf of Mexico is like that. But this resort is being built to withstand hurricanes and to still be eco-friendly. There's a growing market for minimal footprint vacations, I'm told. And Florida is ripe for them."

Liz had, at one point, walked up beside Ian, prompting him to cut short his talk. "One more thing, if you don't mind? When was Nelson Vincenti on the island last? Would Leo know him by sight?"

"He was here briefly two weeks ago, so I doubt Leo would know him. He's returned to London. That's where his head office is. Mrs. Vincenti is due to come next week to visit friends in Fort Myers, so I imagine Mr. Vincenti will accompany her. He'll want to see how the buildings have survived a storm."

Ian knew Annette Vincenti was due to come. He was supposed to have several program proposals ready for her. He thanked the chief, who promised to call the minute the police arrived, and with that, Ian steered Liz away.

"Let's go back to Moss Point."

Liz followed him onto the trail that led from the stream to the spring and then to the trailhead. As they approached the end, Ian stopped and turned to her. "I need to find Monica."

"Why? Do you think she killed that guy? Ian, if it's to turn her over to the police, first we need to talk to her—"

"No." Ian worked his jaw, then added, "There is one other thing that troubles me. Monica needs money—a lot of it. And I don't know if you heard, but—"

"Yes, I heard. The petty cash box was stolen from the resort. How would she be able to steal a cash box? She'd have to know where it was, and as a woman, she'd stand out at a construction site, even if she did work there."

"I know. It doesn't make a lot of sense, but it's the only lead." He stopped abruptly. "A pair of pants was stolen, too. Maybe she dressed like one of the workers. She's about the same size as Leo, and Leo's working there."

She pressed her lips into a thin, skeptical line. "I don't know. She seems awfully feminine to me."

"She's reserved. Maybe because of her background. She came to Florida as a refugee from Central America with her parents when she was a little girl. She told me they'd had no contact with their homeland after that and that her family was very private. That's all I know of her right now, but you can rest assured, I'll know more by this time tomorrow."

"So there's no obvious reason why she'd need the money. Do you think she has a drug habit? Maybe she broke into the clinic looking for drugs?"

"I don't know enough about her. But I've learned that things are sometimes not what they appear. People sink to the lowest points, people who you wouldn't expect."

"We should also find Leo. Smith may have lied to him but then again maybe Leo lied to us."

"*We* aren't going to find anyone. Let me deal with Monica and Leo. But not until after the police arrive. If either of them have something to do with Smith's death, I don't want to tip them off beforehand."

With that, he turned and stalked out the end of the trail and into the area near the front of the rec center.

Just then, a police car rolled to a stop in front of them. Ian introduced himself. They'd been on their way here to respond to the breaking and entering, and were hurried along by the murder. They talked briefly for a moment, Ian learning that the FBI were also on their way, and the officer said he was only too glad to turn the investigation over to them. They wanted a quick look at the rec center before heading to the beach. With a federal case starting a quarter mile away on the beach, the police asked that the center be left as it was until the FBI looked at it, and the security guard agreed to stay.

Over an hour later, Liz and Ian were finished and were allowed to leave. To Ian, the air was depressing, heavy, hot and thick with impending rain. The police said they were expecting the call to evacuate, because Sandy, as the storm was now called, had strengthened quickly.

"I have some information that needs to be distributed in case of a hurricane," Ian told Liz. "I took it home with me last night. I'll need to dig it out and photocopy it."

She nodded. "I'll help."

"And I'm hungry," he added. He imagined Liz was, also. All they'd eaten today was a bit of breakfast and the granola bars he'd taken late this morning after Charlie had been bandaged and sent back with Elsie.

"I don't feel much like granola bars or juice," he said quietly. "But I make a mean tuna sandwich, if you're interested."

She lit up. "I love tuna."

They walked down to his house, Liz pausing at the Wilsons' house for a moment. The curtains were drawn, with only a lamp on in the living room to counter the cloudy evening.

Along the side of the house, Ian noticed Charlie's bedroom light still glowing. He came to stand beside her. The warm sea breeze felt burdened with rain as the evening dragged into night. The wind had increased, its whooshing howl now almost hurting the ears.

"I've been gone most of the day. I wonder how Charlie is," Liz mused.

"Elsie would have called us by now if he'd suffered any ill effects. You can go if you want to, but I need to check my messages and the position of the storm."

"No, I'll check later. If I go in, he'll want me to stay, and Elsie will want to feed me. I'm already a burden to her."

"You're not. But instead of eating her great food, how about you make the sandwiches while I search for those papers?"

She smiled at him, however brief the warm expression was. "Deal."

Ian walked ahead and unlocked his side door. It opened easily, and he stepped into the dark house.

He was shoved hard into the kitchen counter. As he grappled for his balance, he watched a black-clothed body race toward Liz.

SEVENTEEN

Ian leaped to his feet and dove at the man. Both men went down hard, but his assailant twisted about and kneed Ian in the stomach. Air whooshed out of him as he collapsed backward.

Liz jumped backward away from the man, and in a single movement, she grabbed the nearest thing on Ian's counter—a wooden banana stand—and swung it at him. The man ducked, and Liz twirled wildly until she hit the doorjamb with her small improvised weapon.

On his feet in the next second, Ian plowed into the burglar, driving him to the ground. He grappled at his opponent's hair but found it covered in soft cotton. His fingers plucked elastic at the ear.

They flipped and rolled across the room until Ian saw a blur of dark metal slash across his face, blinding him with a burst of pain a moment before a hit to the abdomen knocked the wind out of him.

Over the pain, Ian could hear Liz gasp and cry out. He tried to focus through his watering eyes.

The man shoved Liz and disappeared out the door. Ian collapsed back onto the cool linoleum.

His eyes shut and his face stinging, Ian heard the door slam and felt a warm hand on his shoulder. "It's okay. He's gone. We're both safe. I called the police."

"Did you see who it was?"

"No. I think he was wearing a hoodie and a surgical mask. It's dark in here. Just a sec." She stood and fished around for the light switch. Now flicked on, the light glared in his face. Again, Liz dropped to the floor. "You've been hurt. Let's get you up and into the bathroom."

With her help, Ian rose. Once upright, he walked with her to the bathroom where he peered in the small mirror above the sink. "He hit me with a gun, so I should be grateful he didn't fire it at me." He looked through the mirror at her. "Looks like we're a matching set now."

Liz grunted out something and took a facecloth to wet it. Ian gasped when she pressed the cold, wet cloth to his welt. "It's bleeding a bit. Much worse than mine," she said.

He leaned forward, one hand pressing the cloth and the other gripping the cool porcelain. He shut his eyes.

"Do you think that was Monica?" she asked quietly. "Though Monica is strong, I doubt she's strong enough to take you on, even with the element of surprise."

Ian dabbed his scrape. "Probably not. I was just thinking of all the evidence building up against her. Besides, whoever it was felt too muscular for a woman." He peeled away the cold cloth and rinsed it before reapplying it. "What we need to do is find out what was taken. Let's go."

"Wait, what about your cut? You need to get it looked at. At least let Elsie—"

"No, not right now. We need to discover what, if anything, is missing. Monica took some of the info I had on Charlie, so if that's missing it most likely was her, having come here to get what she thinks is the rest."

"Did you bring it home with you last night?"

He nodded. "I did. I'd been hoping to read through it more and see if there was anything I'd missed before."

By then, they had reached the spare room. When he'd been given this house, most of the furniture came with it. Ian had already given away the spare single bed, among other things, to the couple down the road who'd taken in their grandchildren. All that remained in this room was a battered desk and wobbly chair. Ian had set it up as a secondary office. His laptop remained closed, but the papers he'd brought home were scattered about.

They spent the next half hour sorting through his papers. Just as Liz handed him the last of her pile, his cell phone rang.

Ian answered it with a curt hello. It was the FEMA's office. After talking briefly, he hung up and sighed.

"What's wrong?"

"The island is being evacuated. We have until tomorrow morning to get out. The roads will be closed by then."

He looked grim. "Sandy is now a category one hurricane, and is coming this way. But the police can't get here right away. There are some serious accidents caused by the evacuations."

Liz beat down the fear and tension that seemed to drill into her after Ian's phone call. They had to leave, and Ian said the FEMA wanted them out by tomorrow. His call to the construction site followed, and as Ian patted his cheek and looked down again at the facecloth, he added, "We'll be easier to evacuate than the resort, which has trailers that will need to get hooked up and shipped out of there. But with several of the men needed there, it's going to be tough for the families to move."

"They'll be fine. Mothers have been taking care of families for thousands of years. Let's focus on the village and let the resort handle itself."

Liz watched Ian nod. Then, taking away the face-cloth he'd had plastered on his face, she said, "I'll rinse this out while you start getting that information you need to copy and hand out."

He looked at her grimly. The bloodied welt was darkening, a long slash across his cheek and the bridge of his nose, its deepest part in the soft flesh under his left cheekbone. The gouge would leave a scar, she was sure.

She bit her lip, feeling helpless and foolish and feeling her own welt throb in sympathy. Would any of this have happened if she'd done as Ian wanted when she first got here? She should have asked Charlie to try to look at the pictures and tell them what he'd seen that night his father was killed.

Because she didn't want Charlie hurt anymore, she'd opened the door to all of this—a murder, attacks on each of them, break-ins, fear, pain. Was Charlie's emotional health so fragile that it couldn't stand a short time of pain, compared to all that had happened so far?

She wasn't sure anymore.

"We need to distribute this information to everyone. Plus the bracelets." At his waist, his phone buzzed. He read the message. "Text message. It's a new system where all first responders are alerted via texting about evacuations."

He handed her the papers before he bent to pull out a small steel suitcase. From it, he removed sheets of bar-coded straps. She looked into the suitcase and saw several scanners.

"What's all that for?"

Ian closed the suitcase and hefted it up. "Not too many people have cell phones here. The elderly couple down the road don't, nor do the Callahans. Elsie and George have one to share. So texting out information doesn't work. We need to keep track of the people and their personal effects, like suitcases and medication. We give each person a bracelet like you get at the hospital, and with them comes matching tags for luggage and family members, and we scan them."

Liz nodded. "That makes sense. Have the bar codes already been inputted into the scanner?"

"Yes. It's all ready to go. The other scanner I have is for fingerprints. That usually takes place at a checkpoint and not a village, but we're so isolated here that they gave it to me now. It's the same system used at Disney World."

She chuckled. "At long as it works."

"It does. It also helps to identify felons and such who should be separated from the general population for everyone's safety."

Her smile fell away. "What's next?"

"We need to make sure everyone gets a bracelet and a flyer with information. By now, most people will have received a text message or phone message saying they need to evacuate. Also, I need to move my SUV. It holds eight, so we'll be taking whoever can't get off the island by themselves."

He paused, then pulled out his gun, flipped it around to offer her the grip first. "Take this."

She held up her hands. "What? I don't know how to use a gun."

"Here, look at this."

She tried to listen intently to how to arm the gun, or cock it as he said, even where the safety switch was. And how to hold it when aiming.

"Two hands, no Hollywood stuff," he said.

As if an afterthought, Ian dug through a bottom drawer and pulled out a leather belt. He strapped it around her waist, pulling it to the very last loop. Still, it hung down but didn't slip over her hips. On the side was a holster, and he showed her how it sat in there.

"Are you sure about this? I may end up killing someone."

"But you'll have something to defend yourself with. There is someone here who has already killed a man."

"What about you?"

"I'll be fine. It's in case we get separated."

She gasped. "What if I shoot you?"

"Try not to." He tilted his head, his expression so incredibly serious. Suddenly, he pulled her close and allowed his lips to hover just above hers.

"Think of this as added incentive for you not to kill me," he whispered.

EIGHTEEN

He kissed her hard on the lips. A warm, passionate kiss worthy of her going limp in his arms. And kissing him back.

When he pulled back and lifted his head, he murmured, "At least I hope it has added incentive and not a reason *to* shoot me."

She felt her face heat up. "Oh, yes, that is incentive *not* to shoot you, all right."

But still, as Ian turned away, she couldn't help but remember that they could also be evacuating a killer as well. Would she have to shoot them?

Please, Lord, be with me. She hugged herself. "I feel as though things are coming at me too quickly."

He opened his kitchen door and peered out into the darkness. "Sometimes they do. Sometimes God throws things at us just to get our attention."

"If this was happening two days ago, I'd have been telling you off and demanding I take Charlie and go. But now…everything's so mixed up. Things are changing."

He nodded. "I know you want to leave right now, but there's really no place to go until the shelters get organized. All the hotels and motels will be either full or boarded up."

"We should have left ages ago." She pursed her lips and fiddled with her hands. "I understand why we can't now, but before, you were so adamant for us to wait. Wait for another agent, wait for this and that. You were determined to protect Charlie by yourself."

He didn't answer. Instead, he checked the outside.

Suddenly, she needed to know the truth about Ian. To help him, to follow him, to understand him. "Why, Ian? Why is it important? Because you can bring down some big drug cartel?" She studied him carefully. "No, that's not it. This is personal, isn't it?"

Ian hooded his eyes, looking down. She couldn't catch the expression in them. And yet, she needed to so very much. Just to understand.

"Ian? Why is it personal?"

Finally, he answered, "Because I saw myself in Charlie. I could see him being shuffled around foster homes, relatives, anyone who would take him for a few months. After my parents died, that happened to me. I didn't want him to end up like that. I wasn't an easy teen to raise, and nobody wanted me. That's partly why I didn't want you to grab Charlie and go. In a few years, he'll be too tough to handle."

She opened her mouth to argue back, but Ian wasn't finished. "Maybe that's why I joined the U.S. Marshals. They wanted me when nobody else did."

His words were rushed and forced, as if getting them out was a painful chore. With a quick swallow, she studied her fingernails. They were short, no nonsense, strong, yet well shaped. Not at all the way she felt. But easier to think on than the present situation. In fact, it was *way* easier, knowing a bit about what drove Ian. "I won't leave until I know that I've done all I can do to help Moss Point prepare." She groaned. "I just feel like I'm drowning. Like I can't handle this. And now I'm thinking, how could I expect to look after Charlie when I was so scared right now?"

Satisfied no one was near, he gathered his things together. "You're afraid you're not prepared, that's all. I think every new parent in the world thinks that at some point or another. You just have to have faith."

She lifted her eyebrows. "Faith? In myself? Ian, I know you've given me your gun, and you're showing an incredible amount of faith in me, but I'm not so sure it's a good idea. You didn't think I should leave with Charlie because you didn't think I could handle the responsibility, so don't deny it. Now isn't much different."

He set down his things and reached forward to free up a thin, curly strand of her hair that the wind had thrashed across her face and tangled on her damp forehead. His warm fingers brushed her skin, bringing even more color to them than what the bright sun had already brought.

"Yes, I doubted you. And maybe I was wrong to do so. But all you need is faith. We all need faith."

"Faith in what? My abilities? I have no skills whatsoever! I can capture a bald eagle, but that skill isn't going to get me far here, is it?"

"You can catch an eagle?" he asked, distracted for the moment.

"Yes, and it can be dangerous work. A mature bald eagle can break a person's arm just with its wing. One female cracked my forearm bones once. I've since learned the proper technique for subduing them."

"An eagle broke your arm? In the wild?"

"No, in the eagle house where she was recuperating. It was the day we were to move her back to her hilltop home. I was in a hurry, and the bird wasn't cooperating. Eventually, she was caught and released, but I learned you need patience and strength to subdue them. Especially the females, which are larger than males." She paused. "The point is, I think that now you're putting more confidence in me than is warranted."

He scooped up the metal case again. "No, I'm not. You need faith in God. You're scared right now, but remember that nothing is impossible with God. And He loves you enough to want to give you good things. Things that will bring glory to Him. By you just trusting in Him and in yourself, you can achieve great things for God." He peered outside and then looked back at her. "I'm not talking missionary, pastoral stuff here. I'm talking about you overcoming your fears and doing it with God's help. That will glorify Him, too." He smiled briefly at her. "Just trust Him, okay?"

There was that inner strength she so admired. Liz shut her eyes for a moment, biting her lips and holding back the tears that seemed to want to spring forth without reason.

What would it feel like to share a family with Ian, to help him heal from the pain he'd felt as a child? Would he open up more about his past? Would he impart strength and wisdom to his children, to be the father Charlie needed and the husband she wanted? Even though he seemed to crave the role of U.S. Marshal again?

She felt Ian's fingers wrap around hers. Even in this doorway, listening to the increasing drill of the wind, she could feel the storm pressing closer. It was unlike anything she'd ever felt before. Yet, she remembered Ian's strength.

"Have faith, Liz," he whispered. "Have faith in yourself."

The intensity and the warmth in his voice spoke something different. It was something more than comfort, more than a pastor telling a parishioner to believe—to be strong and trust God.

Liz found herself shifting into his arms. She clung to him again, opening her eyes to stare at him with a searching she couldn't even understand herself. He still gripped the case as he wrapped his arms around her.

And without any conscious thought, they closed the space between their lips. They kissed.

Faith, he'd said she needed. But how could she have faith in herself? What could she do that would muster such faith? She'd failed Charlie several times since his mother died. If she'd only been successful, pushed a little harder, saved a bit more money for a good lawyer, she might have won custody of him and spared him from seeing his own father murdered. Faith was plenty in hindsight.

Yet, right now, with the wind banging the door against the siding, all she wanted was to be in Ian's arms, drawing comfort from him in a way only he could offer it.

What did that say about her? She should be fighting for Charlie's safety, not cringing in Ian's arms, hoping for their kiss to last.

She shifted away from him, gently. A slow smile appeared on his face as he said, "Sorry. I guess I got a bit greedy."

What could she say to that? Breathless, she smiled back.

He kissed her briefly one more time. "We need to start the evacuation. They're giving us twelve hours maximum. I don't want to wait until the last minute. And the sooner Charlie and you are off the island, the safer you'll be."

Ian and Liz quickly delivered the pamphlets to whoever was home. They reached everyone but Monica and the Callahans.

The family who'd taken in the Callahans said that they had already left. They'd left before suppertime. And Monica was nowhere to be found.

"That's strange," Ian mused as they hurried away from the house. "We need to ask Elsie what Jenny and Leo said to her. Leo should have been at work."

When they returned to the Wilsons' house, the first thing Liz did was relinquish the handgun and belt. "I know it was just in case we got separated, but please don't give it to me again, okay?" Ian strapped on the belt and then walked inside.

Elsie reported that Jenny Callahan had come and retrieved her son, saying that they weren't taking any chances and were getting out while the weather was still okay. But she'd said little else of consequence.

"Let me know if you hear from them, okay?" Ian requested.

"I doubt I will," Elsie answered, in a cautious tone. "They don't have a cell phone. And all Jenny said was that Leo had made the hotel arrangements. She didn't even know where they were going or how they'd get there. She was too busy packing. But I'm sure they'll be fine."

Ian exchanged a quick look with Liz.

For the rest of the evening, Liz and Elsie packed, all the while keeping talk to a minimum. Liz wanted to check the television, but Elsie suggested it would rattle Charlie if he saw too much of the storm, so they kept it off. At bedtime, Charlie practiced his reading using a battered old primary reader from years gone by, until, with a hug, Liz told him he needed to go to sleep.

"Prayers, too, Auntie Liz. We gotta say our prayers."

She nodded and knelt down beside him, knowing fully well his sudden piety was partly a delaying tactic.

But hadn't Ian talked about faith earlier, telling her she needed to have faith? She only had to ask God to help her.

Help me with my unbelief, someone once asked of Jesus.

As Charlie scrolled through a litany of things to bless, Liz shut her eyes and thought again of Ian's words. He'd admitted to questioning her ability to parent Charlie. And yet, with kind words, he suggested all she needed was to pray.

Lord, I need help. Help me strengthen my faith. Help me help Charlie and myself. And to bring glory to You.

Yet, her thoughts strayed to Ian—his firm, strong embrace; his soft kiss; and his powerful words. Could she, should she, even, get involved with a man who'd questioned her abilities and would never give up the world he'd created here?

She wanted wisdom, so how wise were her growing feelings for Ian? Would she have to leave Ian here once she was given wisdom?

"And God, take care of Stephen. Cuz I miss him and we didn't get the buried treasure that was gonna help his family build a new house."

Liz listened to Charlie pray. Finally she stood and insisted that Charlie end his miles-long prayer.

"I miss Stephen, Auntie Liz."

"I know. But when the storm is over, he'll be back." She swallowed a tight knot in her throat.

She just couldn't bring herself to tell Charlie that they wouldn't be coming back. The threat to his life was over, and there was no need for WITSEC anymore.

No need to be here, complicating Ian's life. And her own.

With a shaky kiss on Charlie's moist forehead, she pulled the light sheet over him. It was hot in the bedroom. The wind still howled outside, and they'd been forced to shut the window to stop the gale from blowing everything around.

After quietly shutting the bedroom door, she walked over to the kitchen. Elsie and George were busy there and declined Liz's offer of any help. She walked outside to find Ian driving an old SUV out to the front of his house. She waited until he had parked it at the front of his house and come close to her.

The wind had increased, tossing about his short sandy hair and buffeting his loose shirt. Strange to feel such a hot, wet wind, still with no rain, she noted. This whole storm business was so different from the nor'easters that rolled through Maine. They usually brought snow—and lots of it. The wind would be bitter and power would be lost, and all that she could do was bank the fire in the woodstove and crawl into bed with an extra blanket.

"Are you loading up now?" she asked him as he approached.

"Just with a small bit of personal stuff. I need to pack up some stuff from the office, too. There are things there I can't afford to lose. If I do, 'The Shepherd's Smile' could be set back as much as a year. We can't afford that."

He sounded like he belonged here, as if he was here for the long haul, the rest of his life. Why shouldn't he think that way here? The lifestyle was simple here, uncomplicated until she arrived.

And where was she to be? Tomorrow she would leave with Charlie, to a shelter, and then, hopefully, home with Charlie, to start again.

But one thing was certain. She couldn't stay here. She'd overstayed her welcome with the Wilsons, who couldn't afford to have her for too long. And Ian needed to focus on his work here.

But before that, he needed to decide if he should return to the U.S. Marshal Service. Whether or not he realized it, he needed to make that decision. Even she could see that.

"I'll let you go, then," she told Ian softly.

As she turned, Ian caught her arm. She looked down at it, then up to his face, giving him the barest shake of her head. Her lips formed the word *no,* but she couldn't speak it.

His expression hurt, Ian dropped his arm, and she hurried back into the small home.

The next morning, all four of them in the little house were up before the sun. Not that the sun could be seen. Nothing was seen out the windows, thanks to the heavy plywood boards Ian and George had installed. Late last night, the FBI had come by for Liz's statement. But even they were anxious to get off the island.

All night long, the wind had howled, and only Charlie got the sleep needed. With the dim daylight came the inevitable proof that they needed to get off the island immediately.

George said he would check out Monica's house and the family at the end of the road. With Charlie's help, Elsie packed up what food she had cooked last night into a cooler, knowing that if the power went out she'd lose everything in her refrigerator and freezer.

"Auntie Liz," Charlie asked over his cold cereal while everyone bustled around him, "can I call Stephen?"

"Not yet, sweetie. I don't know where they are right now, and once the storm passes, we'll all be back." She still couldn't tell him that from the shelter she would take him straight home.

But he'd make new friends in Maine. There were several boys his age in the village—boys who were anxious to play with other kids.

"You don't need to know where he is, Auntie Liz," he replied, his mouth full of cereal. "You just have to phone him."

Elsie looked up from the papers Ian had dropped off. She was already breaking apart the bracelets with the bar codes on them. "Hon, Stephen's family doesn't own a cell phone."

"Yes, they do!" He glared at both women.

Liz caught a glimpse of the stubbornness her sister had noted once in her husband.

"Why are you so sure they do? Did Stephen tell you they had one?" she asked.

"No. Cuz I saw his dad talking on one yesterday. Stephen said I could call him on it after they left. We could talk about the buried treasure."

Elsie took the bracelet strip and walked around to Charlie. As she wrapped it around his thin wrist, she threw Liz a concerned frown. "Charlie, I don't know Leo's number. We'll have to wait until Stephen calls us. Did you give him your aunt's cell phone number?"

Tears welled up in Charlie's eyes. "I forgot! Auntie Liz, I miss Stephen! I want to see him, but he said his dad was taking them far away! It's not fair!"

Liz sat down beside him, holding out her own wrist so that Elsie could press the bracelet's sticky surfaces together. "Did Stephen's dad say where they were going?"

"I dunno. He was talking on the cell phone about that bad man Ian knows."

Liz froze, her arm still extended toward Elsie to receive her own bracelet, who also froze. "Bad man?"

Charlie looked down at his cereal. "The one Ian has a picture of on his cell phone. The guy I don't like to talk about cuz it hurts."

NINETEEN

Pulling herself together, Liz gathered Charlie up onto her lap, thankful that the boy was still small and lightweight. "I know, sweetie. I know it hurts. And we'll find Stephen, or in a day or two, he and his family will be back."

"Stephen's dad said they wouldn't be back."

She rocked him lightly, her chin resting on the boy's head as he cuddled her. "What else did Leo say?"

"He said that the bad man was still alive, but Leo said he was doin' the talkin' now." Charlie leaned back and stared hard at her. "Auntie Liz, Stephen and I wanted to find the buried treasure, but I think his dad gots it."

Still rocking him, she watched Charlie check out his new bracelet. They said nothing for a long moment, and she wondered what she could say that wouldn't upset him further.

The opportunity came. In typical juvenile fashion, he looked up, and asked, "Can I go on rides with this bracelet?"

She laughed, in spite of the worry churning within her. "Sorry, kid. No fair in town while the storm is going on."

Elsie patted his head, taking the time to check his cut. "Finish your cereal, hon. I have to do the dishes and put them away."

Charlie climbed off his aunt's lap and sat back down in front of his cereal. Liz stood. "I think I'll go see if Ian needs any help. He should be down at the center. If you can spare me, that is, Elsie?"

The woman nodded knowingly. "We'll be fine here. I'll get Charlie to help me bring in those potted plants I have. I'm going to start that right now."

At that moment, a dog howled, his mournful baying cutting through the constant, dull roar of the wind. Elsie frowned. "That can't be Poco! I guess he was out gallivanting when the family was ready to leave."

"Is he going to be okay, Elsie?" Charlie asked, stricken again.

"He'll be fine. If we have room, we'll take him." She smiled, her face losing the deep concern for one brief, bright moment. "I'll have to find a way to put a bracelet on him, though. Maybe on his collar."

Charlie smiled back. "It'll fit his wrist. But I bet he won't like it."

Happy with the silly thought, Charlie returned to eating. Elsie shot a knowing look at Liz. "You should tell Ian about Leo," she said softly.

Liz left in a hurry. The wind shoved her down the stairs, and she had to grip the banister to keep from falling forward. It was hot, incredibly hot, and she was surprised she hadn't noticed it in the kitchen. But boarded windows kept the hot, moist air out.

The gale carried her down to the rec center. Over the wind, she could still hear Poco but couldn't pinpoint his location. It was odd that the Callahans had left him behind.

Odd that they'd left in such a suspicious hurry.

She felt some rain on her face and could taste the salty spray of wind-carried surf on her lips. The trees, even the heavy, live oak in the center of the village, fought the strong breeze. The houses around her were already boarded and abandoned, and the whole village wore a hunkering, fearful feeling.

The wind grabbed hold of the center's front door and threw it wide open. Liz battled with it for several seconds to pull the thing shut.

She found Ian in his office, backing up his work onto the laptop she'd seen in his house. Around him were large plastic containers, some filled and some open. "I'm going to pack the computer in there. But it's too big to take with us. The kitchen is okay, but there are two cases of water to be put in the SUV."

"I'll do that in a second. Ian?"

He didn't look up but stayed focused on his task. "We should have been gone hours ago. Now it's almost too late."

"Don't blame yourself. Have faith."

He frowned, snapped his disks into their cases and set them into the open container. "Turning my words on me, are you?"

"I'm not being mean." She swallowed, struggling to gather her thoughts.

"Good. We are to live by faith not by sight."

She slapped the desk. "Ian!"

Startled, he finally looked up at her.

"We need to talk. Charlie says Leo had a cell phone yesterday and was talking to someone about Smith." Quickly, she related what she'd gleaned from the boy.

Ian considered her words. "He must have Smith's cell phone," Ian stated bluntly. "And I would guess he was talking to Sabby. It sounds like he was brokering a deal for himself with the cartel leader."

"For what reason? For Smith? Do you think he killed him?"

"He could have—" he looked grim "—or else he was planning to—"

Liz gasped, knowing his thoughts were also hers. "To kill Charlie? Or kidnap him? That would be pointless now, wouldn't it? I mean Smith is dead, and everyone else is safe because Charlie can't identify anyone else."

"But think about what Leo said. Charlie heard him say that Smith was alive. He could have been arranging to give them Charlie or to promise to kill Smith himself."

"But that would be pointless. Charlie didn't see anyone but Smith."

"We don't know for sure what he saw. We just know that Smith wanted Charlie dead, and it's likely that the cartel would consider Smith expendable, too. Or perhaps Charlie overheard something that could incriminate the whole cartel."

She didn't need to be reminded of how she refused to press Charlie for his statement. "Either way, Charlie isn't safe anymore, is he?" She gasped. "We need to leave now! Poco is out there howling like a banshee. Maybe he hasn't been abandoned yet! Maybe Leo is here!"

Ian tore around his desk and threw open the door.

"Get in the car!" he ordered as he raced around the SUV. She'd barely shut the door before Ian had the vehicle started and in gear. The SUV spun around in the soft dirt and raced toward the Wilson house.

The screen door was banging wildly in the wind. Potted plants were strewn about. A sense of urgency swept over Liz. The task of moving them would have only taken Elsie a few minutes—less if Charlie and George were helping her.

"The door! The plants!" she cried out as Ian skidded to a stop. "Something's wrong!"

Ian jumped out of the SUV. He galloped up the steps to shove open the side door that led into the kitchen. Close at his heels, feeling her chest tightening and her breath go shallow, Liz also crossed the threshold.

She gasped. Both George and Elsie were lying on the floor of the tiny living room. Blood trailed across George's face to pool on the faded rug, while Elsie lay nearby, as white as a sheet.

Both Liz and Ian dropped to their knees in front of the prone couple. Ian felt for George's pulse and nodded to Liz while she touched Elsie's neck. "She's alive! Her pulse is strong."

Charlie! Liz jumped up and tore down to the small bedroom across from the bathroom, the one she shared with Charlie.

It was empty, as was the master bedroom and the bathroom where two large plants sat on the floor. She cried out his name but received only the howl of the wind in return.

She raced back to the living room, her fear enveloping her.

"Charlie's gone!"

TWENTY

"Leo has taken Charlie!" She stared at Ian hard, her whole body threatening to collapse into tears.

Ian flipped open his cell phone and dialed 911, hating how he was torn into a dozen different directions. But right now, they needed to focus on George. Elsie's pulse was strong, and she was beginning to come around, but her husband wasn't so lucky. And judging by his knuckles, he'd put up his share of the fight.

After reporting what they'd found, not to mention being told who would be answering the call because of the storm, he hung up, then quickly checked George for other injuries before rolling him over into recovery position. The older man remained motionless, his breathing slow and shallow, with a thready pulse that Ian could barely detect.

Elsie groaned, and Liz immediately dropped to the floor in front of her. "Don't move," she warned. "You might have broken something."

"I'm okay," Elsie said, though she needed help to sit up. Looking as though she would swoon again, Liz leaned the substantial woman back against the easy chair.

"What happened?" Liz asked anxiously. "Where is Charlie?"

The old woman's eyes flew open. "He's gone? Oh, mercy, he's not here?" She glanced over at George, who was still prone on the floor. "George! Oh, please, let him be okay!"

"He's been hit on the head, and it looks like he fought back," Ian said, holding a wet cloth to the man's forehead. "What happened?"

"Someone came in and grabbed me from behind. They had a cloth of something horrible smelling." She hesitated a moment, blinking as she touched her face and mouth.

"A type of ether," Ian said. "The nurse keeps some in her clinic for emergency surgeries. She's trained to use it."

"I remember struggling...but that's all." She leaned forward to look worriedly at her husband. "George had gone outside to check the boards on the windows. I had my back to the door. He must have heard me cry out and tried to fight them off."

"Who was it, Elsie?" Liz asked, her voice rising. "Did you get a look at him?"

Elsie shut her eyes a moment, and her lips moved in a silent prayer. When she opened her eyes again, she looked hollow, forlorn and so much older. "It was someone shorter than me, I think. Strong with thin arms. It all happened so fast. Oh, Liz, I'm so sorry we weren't able to keep the boy safe. But God will take care of him. I know He will." She leaned forward, slowly, her hands reaching out to Liz.

Tears now streamed down Liz's face. "I hope so, Elsie. Because I've failed him again. I've failed him like I did before."

Ian felt his heart clench at her words as he rose to rinse a cold compress he'd pressed on George's head wound. They'd all failed Charlie. He was a U.S. Marshal, and even he had failed the boy.

A siren wailed in the distance. It had to be security from the resort arriving first, Ian thought. The mainland 911 dispatcher must have asked them to assess the situation first.

A few more minutes of the cold cloth and George was beginning to stir.

"Lay low, George." Ian leaned forward, his hand resting on the older man's shoulder. "Just for a minute."

The man's mouth moved, his head barely nodding, his eyes half shut, seeming to focus on waking up more than anything else.

They all sat on the floor of the trailer, Liz clutching Elsie's hand tightly and Ian changing the cold compresses every few minutes until the resort staff could arrive. Liz shut her eyes and prayed.

She prayed for Charlie and for forgiveness, for the Wilsons, for the fear eating at her stomach to go away.

"You haven't failed him, Liz," Elsie said softly.

She turned to the older woman, a question showing on her face. Elsie didn't know how much Liz had wanted only to hold on to Ian and how she'd focused too much on that relationship rather than working harder to keep Charlie safe.

"God heard your prayer. You haven't failed Charlie. Bad things happen to us all, some when we're younger than we should be. But you've done all you could for the boy, and children know these things."

She blinked and shook her head. "How could he? You didn't hear what he said to me the day I arrived here. He thought I didn't love him. And look now! I wasn't even around when he was taken."

"Children say lots of things they don't mean. But they know when someone cares for them. They know that even though you can't fix everything that you are there to comfort them. And Charlie knows that about you. You haven't failed him, so stop thinking that."

Elsie studied her husband for a minute, then looked back at her. "Charlie has heard you ask for God's help, and that can give a child a lot of comfort. We are to have faith like a child, and for all that Charlie has been through, he has that kind of faith. Hearing it from you is good for him."

"Jesus told that to his disciples," Liz said quietly.

Liz glanced over at Ian, who knelt beside George. Ian looked up at Liz. He had a pained expression on his face. When her gaze locked with his, Liz saw the look shift slightly, inexplicably, like a frown of questioning. But not quite.

Was he thinking of how she needed stronger faith for Charlie's sake?

Or was he thinking that if they got Charlie back, she'd take him away for good, and he wouldn't get the statement he'd hoped for?

She wasn't sure. All she knew was that he was as worried as she was.

Liz blew out a sigh when she heard the paramedics approach. She was still desperately worried for Charlie, but she couldn't leave the Wilsons while they were alone. They might know something to help Charlie.

But the police were busy, Ian told her after he'd called again. They were warned again to get off the island as soon as possible.

When the ambulance driver asked her what had happened, Liz blurted out, "Leo Callahan has kidnapped Charlie, my nephew! He must have forced his way in here and attacked both of them."

"No, hon," Elsie said, reaching forward to grab her as she began to stand. "George was outside when I was attacked. He raced in here when I kicked over a chair."

George looked across the room at her, ignoring the ambulance attendant who was now bandaging his head. "I was coming back inside. I could hear Elsie call out and knock over the chair. I could hear her attack—"

"Hear who? Elsie?" Ian asked, standing.

"No," George said, pushing aside the attendant's hand for a moment to stare stricken and shocked at Ian. "It was Monica. She attacked us."

TWENTY-ONE

"Monica took Charlie?" The sickening feeling settling in Ian's stomach churned and then flipped when he stood. Monica? "Did she say why?"

George sat up slowly. "She didn't mean to hurt us, Elsie. She was talking wildly, crazy-like, about getting Charlie off the island. Right now."

The paramedic gently pushed George back down, but he was adamant and shoved the man's hands away. "We heard Elsie yell. Monica grabbed Charlie and pushed Elsie to the floor. When she saw me, she knocked me over. I can remember seeing her limping away." He looked down at the blood splattered around him. "This all can't be mine, I hope."

"I don't think it is," the paramedic answered. "You have a nasty gash, but some of that blood is over by the door, even smeared on the jamb. Maybe your limping friend Monica cut herself." He packed away his case. "But if she doesn't show herself in the next little bit, there won't be anyone to come for her. You are the last call we're making before evacuating. And we're taking you two with us," he told George and Elsie. "No arguments."

"I'll be okay—" George started.

"No, way, sir. You may not be." The attendant shot both of them a dark look. "The blows on the head you both received could kill you in a few hours. You both need to be checked out."

Elsie reached over and laid a hand on her husband's arm. "We aren't much good here, George. We'll go to the hospital, and we'll meet them at the shelter as soon as they find Charlie. And they will find him."

George nodded, albeit with a reluctant look on his weathered face. "Fine."

"Yes, we'll find Charlie," Ian announced. "And Monica." Why had she taken the boy?

"She must have been injured," Liz said. "Remember, Poco is out there, upset, and the last time he was upset, he'd found a blood-soaked belt. If she's injured, she may not be thinking rationally."

The paramedics exchanged curious glances.

Liz stood. "We need to find out where she could have taken him." She rubbed her face and found her hand shaking. "Do you think she'd take him to Leo? If he called Smith's boss…"

Ian hauled her close and held her tightly. Then releasing her as he reached behind him for his gun, he added, "I need to call my supervisor. I'll start a search, beginning with Monica's house. You stay here just in case—"

"I'm coming. I need to do something. I can't just give up on Charlie. I won't do that again. I've been scared of failing for too long, and it's not going to happen this time. I *will* find him."

He would have preferred that she go with the ambulance, but a part of him wanted her close. Liz may be able to talk to Monica, woman to woman.

And Charlie trusted her. She had a love for him that was stronger than even some parents' love for their own children. She would be a wonderful mother to him. And he knew it.

A surge of emotion tightened in his throat, but he shoved aside the feelings growing in him. The attraction would be dangerous right now, when he needed to concentrate on the situation. "Let's go." He grabbed Liz's hand and barreled outside.

Incredibly, the wind had risen further.

"Liz!" Elsie called out after the other paramedic helped her to stand. Liz returned to the doorway. "Monica won't hurt Charlie. I've known her for years. I helped her stand on her own two feet after her parents died."

"She has no relatives?"

Elsie shook her head. "Maybe some back in Guatemala but not here. Leo got her a job on that fishing boat he worked on, serving meals to the passengers. She was a good girl."

A glimpse of Ian over her shoulder told Liz that he was close behind her. "We'll go to her house first," he suggested, touching her elbow.

Liz bit her lip. "Charlie told me when he called that the only person here who locked her door was Monica."

"Well, she never used to." Elsie shook her head. "Something's happened to her."

Liz met Ian's eyes when she turned. Her breathing came in shallow gulps, her gaze so fearful and lost that he wondered if she would crumble at any moment.

"Monica locks her doors to keep something hidden," she whispered.

"Or keep someone out," he answered softly, hating the look on her face. He wished with every ounce of his being that he could wipe away her fear.

"A spare house key will be tucked under the bottom of the step," Elsie called out to them. "It may help you find Charlie."

Ian took Liz's damp hand, and they quickly left. The Wilsons were safe with the paramedics, who would soon help them into the back of the ambulance.

A fine mist had started, and over the gale force howl of the wind, he thought he heard a distant rumble of thunder. They quickened their steps, ending up at Monica's house shortly after.

Ian found the key and opened the door. Her house had not been boarded up. The men who'd been nailing the boards donated by the resort hadn't found her to ask her permission, so they'd left it. There were others needing their help.

As a result, the interior was lighter. He turned around in the doorway. "As a U.S. Marshal, I have certain powers of investigation and arrest. I can enter Monica's house but not—"

"Not me? I promise I won't touch anything, but I'm not waiting outside. An extra set of eyes may be just what you need. So don't be thinking of telling me what I shouldn't do."

"I wouldn't dream of it," he answered dryly as he pivoted. By this time they'd entered Monica's kitchen, where Ian called out the woman's name.

All the windows were closed, and some were rattling in the wind. But it was light enough to see. The still, hot air drifting around them told them no one was home. He stepped forward. Not touching anything, Liz followed him. "Charlie? Are you here?"

* * *

No answer, Liz thought dejectedly. She stifled the fear inside of her and rolled over in her mind the same short, urgent prayer she'd been quoting for days. *Keep Charlie safe, Lord. Help us, Lord.*

The kitchen was dark. A few dishes sat in a drying rack beside the ancient sink. Beside the lower cupboard near the door was a pair of ancient rubber boots.

Holding back tears, Liz gripped Ian's hand as they searched the rest of the house. In the tiny bathroom, along the back of the porcelain sink, stood several bottles, swabs and items usually found in a first aid kit. And several bottles and cans containing those unpronounceable compounds Liz had seen on the clinic's list.

"These were stolen from the clinic!"

Ian shook his head. "I don't think she broke into it, though. The back door to the center was smashed in, and all she'd have to do was unlock the front door. I gave her a key."

"But she has these substances."

"Maybe she was given them?"

At that moment, a gust rattled the windows of the house, slashing rain against the glass with angry ferocity. Liz recalled what Ian had said about a storm surge. The whole island could be underwater by this time tomorrow.

Biting back all the insecurities she had, she lingered close to Ian, who was checking out the two minuscule bedrooms.

"Lord, give me strength. Now, please!"

Her prayer was soft, though she'd spoken it aloud. She was also sure Ian had heard it, but he said nothing when he turned away from one of the bedrooms.

"Nothing. We need to check out Leo's home."

They headed over to Leo's house. The front and side windows of the house had been boarded up, but not the ones around the back. Because of the fire, the whole back end wasn't secure. Ian stepped over the charred threshold, followed closely by Liz.

"Charlie!"

No answer. They walked into the kitchen. Over the heat and rain, Liz could smell the acrid, charred scent left by the fire. They walked into the front room. It was remarkably untouched by the damage. In fact, in the dim light, it looked very much like any ordinary living room except there were several blankets and pillows on the floor.

Ian pulled a tissue from his pocket and carefully opened a drawer in a desk by the window. He gently sifted through the contents.

"Look." With his right hand, he held up several papers, printed copies of Web sites that dealt with handling weapons. Liz peered down at the ones still in the drawer. They were lists of various names, plus info on the people.

"These," Ian said grimly, "are copies of confidential docs my supervisor sent me. The only person I know who could have printed them out would be Monica. She had printed out confidential info on Charlie, so she must have somehow found these as well. She knows my password."

"Charlie said something about that." Sick dread roiled in her stomach. "But why give them to Leo?"

She pursed her lips. Think! Where would Monica take Charlie? "They'd need to hide him," she told Ian.

"They wouldn't risk going across the causeway because they'd be spotted. The resort workers will be moving equipment over it all day. And they must realize that staying here would be dangerous. Even the couple who'd hoped to stay left early this morning in the resort van."

"Maybe in the car we found?"

"I thought of that, but I'm betting that Leo sent his family away in it. No. This isn't adding up somehow. Think about how Monica acted around Leo."

"I didn't notice anything strange. What do you mean?" Liz asked.

"I mean she gave him a wide berth, so to speak. When she came to help put the fire out here, she kept throwing him strange looks. And she was in the forest digging in the ground when you surprised her. Shortly after, we meet Leo, who also has dirt under his fingernails. They were both after something buried."

Liz gasped. "The petty cash has been stolen from the resort! I wonder if it was in a strong box like most other places."

"The chief said it was. Someone stole it and buried it, and Monica was searching for it. She must have known about it."

"Smith might have stolen it. Remember, the security chief said some pants were also stolen. At first, I wondered if Monica took them to help sneak onto the resort. But there's no way she could pass for a man. But Smith might have needed them. He'd be better at blending into a construction site than a woman like Monica."

"That doesn't tell us where Leo fits in all of this. And he's got to, you know."

"No, it doesn't. He and Monica are in on something, even though it feels like they don't trust each other."

Liz grabbed Ian. "Charlie mentioned buried treasure, but I figured he was thinking of pirate treasure, but it could be the money. Leo has something to do with the theft, I'd guess."

Logically sorting through the possibilities comforted her. Here was something she could do. Even though it wasn't getting them any closer to Charlie, she knew it was better than doing nothing at all.

On his belt, Ian's cell phone rang. After looking at the screen, he quickly answered it.

Liz watched him pale.

It was bad news.

TWENTY-TWO

Over the roar of the wind, Ian heard the anxiety in Leo's voice.

"Ian, if you want this kid, then come to the beach."

"Leo? You took Charlie?"

"I didn't. It was Monica. I have the kid, and he's pretty scared but okay."

The hairs on Ian's neck rose. Why didn't Leo just bring Charlie back? Why call and ask Ian to go get him?

"Bring him back to the rec center, then. We're all ready to leave."

"I can't. I have some things to do. Monica is acting crazy. You had better come. Both of you."

Oh, yeah, something is up. Leo was a little too anxious. "Just a sec, Leo. I have to get to some-place sheltered. I can hardly hear you." He covered the phone with his hand and hurried to the door.

After opening it, he held the phone into the wind for effect. "It's Leo." He whispered to Liz. "He has Charlie, but this is a trap."

"How do you know?"

"Because he refuses to bring Charlie here. He says he's too busy, and we have to come get him. If he's using Smith's phone, then he has Sabby's private number. Think of it, Liz. The private number for the cartel's big boss. Charlie said Leo told someone on the phone that Smith was alive. As long as Sabby believes that Smith is alive, he believes there is a threat to his cartel. But if someone was to offer to kill you, Charlie *and* Smith, for a price, then that would eliminate any ties to him."

"But I don't know anything."

"You must. Liz, when you were talking about seeing Smith driving from the direction of your house, did you see anyone else with him?"

"No. He was alone."

"When you were in Bangor, at Jerry's apartment? When you were talking about it, you had a look on your face, as if you were trying to remember something. What was it?"

She threw up her hands! "I don't know! Look, Ian, the longer we talk about this, the more danger Charlie is in. I may know something, but it doesn't matter right now! We have to go. We have to take the chance that Leo will let Charlie go. That he *really is* busy and can't bring Charlie."

"He's lying, Liz!" Ian hissed back.

"He has Charlie, and I don't care about his lies. won't abandon Charlie." She glared at him. "And won't drive away from here without him. You may be brewing up some grandiose plan to rescue him, while leaving me here, but that's not going to happen. You need me, because I'm the only one who Charlie will listen to, and we may need him to obey your instructions. So forget telling me to leave or to stay put. I'm going with you."

"I came to that conclusion ten minutes ago." He lifted his brows for effect.

"Oh. Well, let's go!" She took two steps toward the trailhead when Ian yanked her back into Leo's living room.

"We're taking a shortcut. Leo may have an ambush set up. I want the element of surprise. If he has Smith's cell, then he probably has his weapons. And that could include a handgun *and* a rifle."

"Which way, then?" She looked brave, but Ian could see her throat bob, her tongue run over dry lips and he heard her short little sniffle, even over the wind.

He brought his phone to his ear again. "You still here, Leo?"

"What took you so long?"

"Trying to find some shelter. Where are you? Where the spring runoff meets the beach?"

"Yeah, you know the spot. Five minutes." He hung up.

Ian put away his phone. Without another word he pulled Liz out of the house and down the road toward the center. Liz yanked on him. "Where' Charlie?" she asked him.

"He wants to meet us at the beach."

"Why the beach? A storm is coming."

Not wanting to answer, Ian pulled her along the length of the center and right into the thick forest behind it. The vines slapped at them in the gale, and yet, he still kept talking. "He dragged Smith's body there, hoping it would get washed away. Then he decides he'll kill you and Charlie. He would need proof that you were all dead, though, and Smith' body has already been taken."

"He took pictures of it with the cell phone, Ian," Liz yelled at his back. "You have a picture of Smith on your phone."

"Not good enough. Photos are no proof. Wait!" He snapped his fingers. "Smith had a finger missing. I thought that fish had gotten it, but Leo must have cut it off."

Liz wrinkled her nose and cringed. "That's gross, but it's still no proof that Smith would be dead."

"Perhaps Leo thinks that combined with a photo or even a video taken by the phone, would be enough."

"Forget that. I'd rather we focus on getting Charlie. Where are we headed? To the beach south of where Leo thinks we're meeting him?"

"Exactly. Look, the beach is ahead. Let's get down low and be quiet." He yanked her down to a kneeling position.

She lowered her voice. "Ian—"

"Shh."

"No!" She barely raised her voice, and it certainly was hard to hear above the rising wind, but she had to speak. She crawled up close to him. "Are you saying that Leo wants to kill us for the cartel?"

He twisted around, surprised to see her so close. "I don't know anything for sure. All I know is it makes sense." He softened. This was hard for him, a seasoned marshal. He couldn't imagine how hard it would be for Liz. The rain still found them in the thick of the forest, with not only the canopy of trees but also the vines that crawled only a few feet upward. Liz's hair was plastered to her face on the windward side.

She was beautiful—so caring, so trusting, so untouched by the ugliness of the world. He wanted to keep her like that.

But she wasn't untouched. She'd been dealing with Jerry and his disgusting lifestyle for as long as her sister had been with him.

She was strong about it all. Stronger than she realized.

"Liz," he whispered, "we'll get Charlie back. won't allow Leo to hurt a hair on his head."

She bit her lip and nodded.

He turned away from her before he messed up this mission with a foolish kiss. He needed to focus on their task, not on his own distracting desires.

After crawling through the narrow stretch of woods, he finally reached the edge of the beach Unlike some places, where the beach gradually mixed with the forest, here, the beach started abruptly. The forest floor beneath them was soft almost loamy, and gave suddenly to messy sand a narrow skirting around the greenery. He didn' really like it, but where they lay did provide good cover.

He pulled out his handgun and lay prone on the ground, legs splayed around the tree trunks and his hip digging into a small, broken stump. Rain peppered him.

"Is he there?" Liz asked behind him. "Do you see Charlie?"

"No. We're about twenty yards south, and in this rain, I can't see much."

"If you can't see Leo, then maybe he can't see—"

He didn't let her finish. He crawled out on the beach, peering through the drenching rain. Sand was also bouncing up into his face, stinging his eyes, forcing him to blink continually.

"Ian!"

It wasn't Liz calling. The masculine voice, oddly deep for a skinny person like Leo, sliced roughly through the wind and rain. "I can see you, Ian. Stand up or the kid dies."

Ian squinted ahead. Leo was standing not too far off, Ian's night vision goggles dangling around his neck. Ian hadn't checked the bottom drawer of his filing cabinet yet.

Leo had one hand on a gun and the other on Charlie's quivering shoulder.

"And tell your friend, Liz, to stand up, too. I want you both out in the open."

TWENTY-THREE

Landfall, Liz noted as she stepped onto the beach. Already-wild waves slapped fiercely at the thin ribbon of sand. The small sand knoll by the creek was being pounded on one side, while churning waves and beachfront were building the other side up.

The small knoll wouldn't last. Even Liz could see this. The hurricane's east side would carry the brunt of the rain and wind, destroying whatever lay in its path.

Liz felt herself buffeted about and grabbed Ian for support. He held her tightly as he scanned the beach. Warm rain lashed at both of them.

"Auntie Liz!"

The words, weak and scared, made Ian clutch Liz hard to stop her from rushing forward. Ahead, near the rise where the creek battled the surging waters, Leo and Charlie wavered to keep their balance.

"Charlie!" Liz wrenched herself free and raced toward them, stumbling in the soft sand of the deteriorating knoll and falling into the pooling mix of creek and gulf waters.

Ian galloped up beside her. When he met her, he shoved her back away from Leo, who still clung to Charlie. At the same time, he aimed his gun at Leo's head. "Keep back, Liz," he called out. "He could hurt either you or Charlie."

Leo pulled Charlie in front of him, at the same time pressing the gun into the child's temple. The boy froze with fear, his eyes wide, his wet T-shirt fluttering in the increased wind. He looked terrified. Leo tossed back his wet hair with a flick of his head, but the black strands lashed back against his face.

Liz dared a fast look up at the sky. A long band of dark cloud stretched over them, closer then before, heavy with unshed rain. The waves were choppier than she'd seen them in a long time.

Hurricane Sandy was here.

She stared hard at Leo. "Let him go, Leo. He's just a child. What did he do to you?"

"It's what he's going to do for me! This isn't personal. This is about needing money. I've been stuck on this island barely making ends meet for years. I was laid off when the economy collapsed. I swore I'd do anything to get out of this life."

"He's a child. How can he get you out of this life?"

Leo glared at them. "You're not going to get me to say anything more, all right? Monica kept nagging me on that, until I couldn't stand it anymore. She was worse than my wife."

"So you plan to kill us all, and you think you'll get off scot-free?" Ian asked.

"Shut up!" Leo waved the gun around, and Liz's heart tightened in cold, hard waves as she watched Charlie cringe and duck. He kept looking down to his left, then over the hill to where Liz was, kneeling in the sloppy sand.

Then back down to his left again.

Liz couldn't see what he was looking at, not from her position, and she didn't care. All she wanted was to get Charlie out of Leo's evil clutches.

She couldn't stand it anymore. No way would she allow anyone to hurt Charlie ever again. He'd had too much pain in his life. With a growl, she leaped up and yanked Charlie away from Leo's grasp at the very second that the man tried to shove his wet hair out of his eyes.

Charlie was flung forward into her arms, and she swept the boy behind her. She knew she would pay for this insane act of bravery with a bullet, but Charlie would be away from Leo's grasp. If anything happened to her, Ian would care for her nephew and be a very good father to him. She knew that now.

Leo bellowed at her, but Liz ignored him. She found herself staring down at where Charlie had been standing.

Monica was lying there. Even in the rain, Liz could see that the woman was bleeding heavily.

Ian couldn't believe Liz did what he'd just witnessed. She was lightning fast, as fast as a hungry water moccasin striking its prey.

Neither he nor Leo could stop her. After she flung Charlie behind her, Ian reached up, grabbed both of them and shoved them down. Even then, her head popped back up, and she gasped.

And with good reason, he could see. Monica lay there.

Another piece of the puzzle clicked into place, but he still couldn't see the whole picture.

In that moment, as Ian tried to understand what was happening, Leo wrapped his fingers around Monica's upper arm and hauled her limp body up to his thigh. He crouched slightly behind her. She dangled there, her face wrinkling in pain, as Leo shoved the gun to her head.

"You shot her?" Ian heard Liz cry out to Leo.

"And I'll kill her this time, if you don't cooperate." He looked at Ian. "Drop your gun, Ian."

Ian slowly set his handgun down onto the wet sand. His hat bumped in the wind but stayed plastered to his head.

"Good," Leo yelled back. The gale force winds buffeted him so hard that he had trouble staying crouched. Around them, the salty spray and heavy surf pounded them, and one wild wave surged farther than the rest, almost reaching Ian's handgun as it lay in front of him. Ian looked at it, then up to Leo's hardened features.

Leo wanted to kick it into the water, Ian could tell. But he didn't dare move away from Monica. Ian saw her free arm move, her hand grapple at the wet sand beside her. Her expression said so much. Pain, worry and when her eyes fluttered open, they met his.

Regret, too.

Monica scooped up a thick handful of sand and then swung her arm forward in a wide arc.

She flung the sand up at Leo.

Carried by the wind, the sand hit him square in the face, filling eyes and nose and open, snarling mouth. Leo staggered backward, coughing and spitting and growling harshly. With his free hand, he swiped at his eyes wildly.

A flash burst from the end of the gun he held, its loud report ringing all around them. Ian felt the searing impact in his left shoulder, but regardless,

ne sprang forward, his palms snagging the gun in
Leo's grip and shoving it skyward. His arm stung
with incredible pain.

A gust of strong, hot wind, bringing with it a tor-
ent of stinging, salty rain, blew up at that moment,
and both men staggered under the onslaught. With
the wind helping him, Ian grabbed the gun and
turned it on Leo, but the angry man flung himself
forward, blinded by the sand as he rammed into the
short barrel. He grabbed Ian's right hand, trying to
wrench free the gun.

Ian squeezed the trigger, half by his own conscious effort and half by the man's furious grasp
around the gun. Leo was tossed back to land
beside Liz. He didn't move—only the look on his
face turned from rage to shock, then sagged into
nothing.

Ian, in horror, tossed away the gun. He wrapped
his arms around Liz after she scrambled up to him,
ignoring all the pain that came with her grabbing
him firmly.

It didn't match the pain inside of him. *Lord, what
have I done?*

He knew, as God knew. He'd been so convinced
that he could do his job well, without the Lord, and
God had allowed him enough rope to hang—

He'd sunk back into the way he was before he'd
given his life to God—arrogant, prideful. And he'd
killed a man.

He'd given his life to God, given up the duties that sometimes put him in positions of aggression and with his own impudence, he'd slipped right back there again.

"Forgive me," he whispered into Liz's ear.

She set him back. "For what?"

"For being arrogant, thinking I could do this all by myself, without God's help. And now, I've killed a man. That's not why I came to Spring Island."

She shook her head and swept rainwater off his face. It was a useless effort, but he wouldn't have traded the gentle caress for anything. "You came to help people. God knew where this was going to lead, but He also knew it led you back to Him. He saved you, and you saved a lot of people, including Charlie and me and a whole village."

"Charlie!" Ian spun around, cringing and gasping in pain. Where was the boy? Did he have to witness another gruesome crime? If he wanted to be a part of the boy's life from now on, how would Charlie witnessing another murder affect that?

Liz rose and called out the boy's name.

A moment of fighting the wind and rain rolled slowly past. Then Charlie appeared at the edge of the forest. Spotting Liz, he stumbled over to her.

"Where did you go?" she asked him.

"I ran away. I know I wasn't supposed to do that, but I got scared. I don't like Stephen's dad. He tried to grab me in the clinic, but Elsie came in and he stopped."

"Did Elsie see that?"

"No. He stopped when she started to call me. He made me hit my head when I was escapin' him." He looked at the prone man beside them. "What happened to him?"

"He's dead, and he's not going to hurt you, ever." Liz stroked his short, bristly hair. Ian smiled. At some point, he'd lost his glasses. He was glad. They looked terrible on him.

Charlie buried his head into Liz's waist, just as she looked over at Ian. His heart hitched up at her smile.

Her beautiful, patient smile. "Thank you. We couldn't have made it through all of this without you—and God's help."

"With God's help," he added.

"I've learned so much," she answered. "I was so scared I would fail Charlie, that I wasn't trusting that God would use me and my own strengths. Not until Charlie went missing and not fully until now, when I jumped up at Leo. I was trying to subdue him like I was taught to subdue eagles, but I don't think I did it right." Her voice hitched. "But you're injured."

"It's okay, Auntie Liz." Charlie scrambled over to Ian. "I know what to do."

Liz shook her head. "No, honey, we're here to take care of you. No one is going to hurt you."

"I know that. I've been praying like I was taught in Vacation Bible School. Ian said God will take care of me if I love His Son, Jesus." The boy looked earnestly at Ian. "We've got to pray, you know. Like you said, too, on Sunday morning, Ian. Do you remember that?"

Ian frowned. To be honest, he had no recollection of what he'd told the kids or what he'd preached this past Sunday. But then he remembered. Yes, he'd told them all last Sunday, while giving his message, that praying was absolutely the most important thing a Christian can do. A person didn't get to heaven by praying, but it reflected a soul saying that it needed Jesus. That it couldn't be arrogant like he'd been.

Charlie's eyes were tightly closed, his face scrunched up tightly and his hands steepled together so hard his little knuckles were white. "God, you gotta help us here, cuz we don't want anyone to die yet. Make Monica okay, and get Pastor Ian to fix his gunshot wound. Make it better than you did for Dad, okay?"

Charlie's eyes popped open. Then he slammed them shut again. "Amen!" Opening them a second time, he grinned brightly despite the rain. "God heard me, even though it's windy. He knows you two are too busy to pray."

Ian couldn't speak. So much was racing through him, more than just the pain in his shoulder.

"Now that we've prayed, I know what else to do," Charlie added.

Ian peered down at him. The boy was peeling off his wet T-shirt. Through the fog of pain, he rasped out, "What are you doing?"

"Dad let me go to a Cub Scout camp last summer. I learned first aid." A shadow passed over his face. "But I did all I was taught when Dad was shot. It didn't work, though."

Liz crawled around to the windward side to block the rain and wind. "You helped your dad after he was shot?"

"I was with him when he died. Two men came in to my bedroom while Dad was saying good-night. That's when I saw him get shot. At first I hid under the blankets, then I helped Dad. I called the police on Dad's cell phone. Then they started shooting each other."

"Two men?" Ian held his breath. The boy was there when his dad was murdered. For some time, he'd actually begun to wonder if the boy had seen anything at all. *But he had.* He had seen Smith *and* another man. Leo must have gleaned that fact, maybe suggesting it to Sabby.

Sabby had reportedly been seen in the States. Ian sucked in his breath.

Smith and Jerry Troop had been implicated in the attempted assassination of that Guatemalan politician who had the power to destroy the cartels in his country. And they weren't alone in that assassination attempt. Or else because it had failed and Smith was told to eliminate Jerry. This mess could bring down a whole cartel if Jerry or Smith talked. The only solution would be to kill both of them. Had Sabby come to the States to do that, and had Charlie thwarted his plans?

And yet, hot on the theory of what might have finally happened was something more imperative.

The boy had prayed. Charlie had prayed for safety, when his pastor hadn't. He had trusted God for help, when Ian was trying to do it all by himself.

"'Whosoever shall not receive the kingdom of God as a little child, he shall not enter therein,'" he quoted softly from the Bible, knowing the words would be carried away by the wind. "Jesus told the disciples not to keep the children away, because we can learn from their complete faith." He cleared his throat and dropped to his knees.

Lord, what have I been doing? I've been doing it all, without You. Forgive me, Lord, for forgetting You.

He blew out a lungful of air at his major screwup. *How could this have happened?*

Because he'd slipped back into his old role of marshal, returned to a time when he'd foolishly thought he didn't need God. Because he'd wanted to return to the excitement of being a U.S. Marshal.

He had forgotten all the peace he'd received after putting everything in God's hands.

Lord, I need You. I'm sorry for thinking I could do everything without You.

He looked up, finding he was being watched by both Liz and Charlie. Then the agony returned, sharply, as Charlie wrapped his T-shirt over Ian's shoulder to tie off at the back. Ian seethed with the fiery pain as Liz tightened his knot. He blinked and met Liz's contrite expression.

She bit her lip. "Charlie, did you see who was in your apartment?"

Charlie nodded, moving around to Ian's back and focusing on his handiwork with deep concentration. "Both of them. One was that guy on Ian's cell phone. The other had a funny name."

"Never mind!" Ian snapped. "We don't need to talk about any of this right now."

Or ever, he decided to himself. With all that was happening now, Charlie didn't need to rehash the pain he'd been forced to experience. He needed time to heal. He wouldn't force the boy to talk, like he had wanted. He'd find another solution. With God, all things were possible. Have faith.

A light touch brushed his arm, and he looked up to find Liz's watering eyes blinking as she smiled at him. "Thank you."

He swung back his right arm, the one that didn't hurt, behind her and pulled her into him. Their lips touched ever so briefly. Heat burst through his chest. He had so much to be thankful for, himself. *Thank You, Lord. Thank You for bringing me back to You.*

But the danger wasn't over yet. One hard slap of water told them that much. The predicted storm surge was here, and it was very high.

And Sabby still wanted Charlie dead.

TWENTY-FOUR

"We've got to get out of this storm. And off this island," Liz announced forcefully. "With Monica, too." She only hoped that Monica's brave act wouldn't be her last. They needed to get her to a hospital, but the ambulance attendants had said that they wouldn't be returning until after the storm.

"Charlie, you go on ahead and hold the branches back. Ian, can you stand?"

"Yes." He stood, and though she could see the pain ripple over his features, she was forced to fight her desire to hold him. "I'll take Monica's upper body, and you grab her legs."

Together, they managed to carry the woman into the forest.

Liz was grateful that the trees filtered the wind and rain enough for them to get back to the village. As soon as they left the trail behind them—and could see the rec center ahead—a gust lifted Ian's Tilley hat off his head and away into the forest.

That beaten-up old thing was finally gone, she thought. The SUV still sat there, and Charlie ran ahead to open one of the back doors. They managed to slide Monica onto the back bench seat. Amazingly, Charlie crawled in with her, grabbed one of the blankets shoved behind the seat and draped it over her.

"You gotta keep her warm," he told Liz.

As she leaned forward to help Charlie, a hand clamped on her arm.

"Liz?" Monica said weakly.

Liz lowered her head toward the woman. "Yes?"

"I'm…sorry. I need the money. I…wanted you to leave."

Liz sat back, her head lifting to meet Ian's pained expression. She leaned forward again. "Don't speak. We'll talk when you're better."

"Will God forgive me?"

Ian pushed forward, gritting out through his agony. "Yes, Monica. God forgives you."

Not wanting to waste any more time, Liz jumped into the driver's seat and started up the vehicle. Ian climbed in beside her more slowly. Abruptly, a dog barked and scratched at the SUV. On the passenger side, Charlie opened the door. Poco jumped in.

The road to Northglade was empty, except for one lone police officer who let them through and contacted the Northglade Health Care Center. Thankfully, a skeleton staff had remained on duty and took Ian and Monica in immediately.

Sitting ramrod straight in the waiting room, stroking Charlie's hair as she listened to the wind howl and the rain slash at the front entrance, Liz prayed—for the strength she knew God would give to her and mostly for Ian and Monica. Both had gone too long with a bullet hole, ripping muscles and sinew and losing too much blood.

A nurse appeared. "Liz? Ian's asking for you."

Liz rose. Seeing that he had dropped off to sleep, she wondered where she could leave Charlie.

"Here, give him to me," the nurse said, holding out her arms. "I'll put him in the room beside your friend's."

"Thank you." Liz followed the nurse down the hall and watched her gently set him down on the bed in another room and cover him with a blanket. She then followed the nurse down the empty corridor, quiet except for the raging storm outside.

"How is Monica?" she asked the nurse.

"She's been taken to Miami by ambulance," the woman answered over her shoulder, "but she regained consciousness and seems pretty strong. She'll pull through. She said a lot of things that don't make any sense to me, but they might to you."

Ian was in the first room on the left. Half of his chest and all of his left shoulder was bandaged up. With an IV in his arm and a tired look on his face, he smiled at her.

"Everyone okay?" he asked.

"We're fine. Charlie's sleeping, and I talked to Elsie, who said everyone is safe at the high school, even George. Monica is on her way to Miami, but the nurse says she'll be fine."

He agreed with her. "She told the nurse a few things. She was in debt, as I knew, but she spent it on trying to find her sister, who had been left in Guatemala. The family couldn't get her out when they left, and she disappeared shortly after."

"So she stole the petty cash from the resort?"

"No, she said that Leo claimed to have stolen it and was going to give her some money if she would find out about Charlie for him."

"Leo knew about him?"

"Not at first. But Monica said she was told that Smith saw Leo steal the money and found him in the forest burying it and threatened to tell security at the resort unless Leo could get him Charlie. Leo must have been shocked, getting discovered by a strange man in the forest and then extorted by him."

Liz took Ian's hand and held it. "So, he was willing to part with some of the money for information."

"Yes. I think Leo wondered why Charlie was worth so much and what I knew. Leo asked Monica to access my computer for the info, because she was desperate for money, and later, he asked her to help him get Charlie. But I think she refused."

"She must have realized the situation was getting dangerous. When I caught her in the forest digging, she must have been looking for the box. That's when she told me to leave with Charlie. I wonder if she was planning to leave with him."

"She said something the nurse couldn't catch, something about a snake, so I'm betting she was the one who put the snake in your luggage in order to scare you off."

"Where does the fire at the Callahans' fit into all this?"

"Monica told the nurse about Smith threatening Leo and that Leo was 'ripe for revenge.'"

Liz gasped. "So Leo killed Smith?"

"No proof yet, but Monica claims she heard it. It wasn't until she saw the belt that she realized what Leo had done to Smith. I'm thinking Smith set the fire with the hopes of scaring Leo into helping more. Smith didn't dare show himself in the village, and at night, George and I shared shifts to keep an eye on the Wilsons' house."

"Poco got very upset on two occasions. One right around the time Smith was murdered," Liz answered thoughtfully. "And the other could have been when Leo shot Monica. She must have been a threat to him."

"I bet she refused to help anymore, and when she heard about Smith's murder, Leo decided she'd have to die, too. Good thinking about Poco. I hadn't considered that he'd be a witness, of sorts."

"I think he smelled blood in the air, and with everyone anxious, he was upset, too. But I wonder who tried to run me off the road."

"Smith. Leo would have been working, and the security chief didn't mention he'd been dodging work. But fingerprint tests may prove that, when we locate the car. And that's just a matter of time. The nurse also listened to Monica say that she meant to take Charlie off the island to save him but was intercepted by Leo. She said something about Leo breaking into the clinic to get stuff to clean himself up. I think that he also took the ether Monica used on Elsie."

"Why?"

"To give to Monica to subdue Charlie, but instead, she tried to steal Charlie off the island."

Liz paused. "Leo must have been thinking that he could make more money than what he stole from the resort, by talking to the big boss at the cartel. But first he decided to kill Smith. He wasn't thinking straight, was he?"

"The fire and nearly losing his family must have upset him. After he killed Smith, he found the phone and called the cartel with his plan to give them the two of you. You're right, though, he wasn't thinking straight. He'd killed the guy he needed to be alive. That's why he told them Smith was alive, just as Charlie overheard."

"His poor family. He must have sent them away in that car we found, and now they have no father and maybe don't even know it."

"'The Shepherd's Smile' will take care of them."

"Do you think he was the one who broke into your home?"

"I think so. I bet that if we searched his house properly we'd find the jacket and surgical mask."

She stepped closer to him. Outside, the wind rattled everything, and the roar was deafening. "Enough of this. You need to get some rest. Any questions can wait until tomorrow."

"Liz, there are some more things that can't wait."

"There's nothing, Ian—"

"No, hear me out. I took the position with 'The Shepherd's Smile' because I wanted to do good things for the people of Moss Point. And I took that last assignment with the U.S. Marshal Service because I figured I could do it all. You've taught me that I can't and I shouldn't. You also taught me about sacrifice."

She lifted her brows. "Sacrifice? How?"

"How you were willing to do anything for Charlie, even when you didn't think you could. You were willing to risk it all for him. That's bravery. To face trouble even when you're scared."

"I hadn't thought about that."

"That's why I love you."

Before her bravery faded away, Liz leaned down to kiss his lips. He pulled her closer and kissed her hard back. When she lifted her head, she whispered, "I love you, too, Ian. So very much."

She curled up beside him and stared up at the ceiling, forgetting for the moment the storm raging, the terrible tragedies and no matter how much they may love each other that there was still a gap of about a thousand miles between them. She lived in Maine, and he was a man on a mission here. She wasn't mission material, and would Charlie want to stay here, a place with such terrible memories? She had to think of him.

"Liz?"

"Yes?"

"We need to discuss other things. I know I've agreed to administer 'The Shepherd's Smile,' but if you don't think it's best for you and Charlie, and you want me in your lives, I'll tell the Vincentis I

have to leave. Many good pastors could do my job.
I want to marry you. I want to spend the rest of my
life with you."

"You would do that for us?"

"If you want me, I would. I trust you, and I know
you seek the Lord's will in all things. I can see that."

Tears sprang in her eyes. "I try to. I always
thought I wasn't strong, but you've shown me that
I am." She paused. "But I don't know about Charlie.
He may not want to stay here. There have been so
many awful things happen to him here. Is it right
to keep him here?"

Something hit her hard on her right side, the one
not touching Ian. "No, Auntie Liz, let's not leave
Moss Point! Please! Not ever!"

She bent her head down, and seeing a short scruff
of bleached hair at her elbow, she sat up. Charlie
clung to her legs, and with pleading eyes, he stared
up at her. "I don't want to leave Moss Point! I mean,
your home is fun and all, but I like it here. I like Ian
and George and Joseph and all my friends here. I
don't want to leave them."

"You said it was too hot here."

"We'll buy an air conditioner. We'll borrow Elsie's
fan. It'll be okay. Let's not leave, okay? Okay?"

Liz smiled at Ian. "I'm beginning to see that
the Lord wants us both down here. Out on Spring
Island, building a church."

"There may not be much of an island when we get
back. The storm surge could swallow it all up."

"Then we'll be helping the community rebuild itself."

Ian's cell phone rang and he grimaced as he answered it. Liz stayed close. Finally, after he hung up, Ian lay back and spoke. "Because of Leo's call to Sabby, the police were able to trace him. They arrested him at a New York airport, trying to leave. And they have enough evidence to charge him with Jerry's murder."

She looked down at Charlie. "Is hearing this sad for you?"

"Nope. God keeps me safe everywhere, even when I act up. So I have to stay here cuz it's part of the deal I made with God. I stay here and tell Ian about the men who killed my dad and God will make sure I don't get hurt anymore. That's the deal I made with Him. He'll take care of you again, and make you strong, too. We'll lift weights together to help."

Laughing, she squeezed him close, as Ian squeezed her close. "So where else can I learn about God and His love but with a pastor husband and a boy who loves the Lord, too? In a village that teaches us so much?" She met Ian's lips with her own and shut her eyes.

The storm blasted on, and she could hear the nurse talking in the hall about the hurricane.

But they were all safe and together. In love.

* * * * *

Dear Reader,

As someone who lives in a cold climate, I love to vacation down south. Naturally, the hot summer weather I avoid, but I often thought of those who must make that transition. And of course, I think of how exotic even Florida seems to me and how I would love to set a story where the heat practically becomes a character in the story.

But it's more than just a story set in hot weather that drove me to write *Silent Protector*. Children touch our lives all the time, and when they are in danger even childless adults are willing to die for them. It's something I believe God has set in our souls. And as a writer, putting a child into a story is a joy. They are so innocent, so sweet, it's wonderful to write them. So when they are put in danger, the tension ratchets up in exciting increments. I hope you feel the same way Liz and Ian feel when they learn to work together, find love and save those who mean so much to them.

Barbara Phinney

QUESTIONS FOR DISCUSSION

1. Once he starts talking, Charlie sometimes tries to talk his way out of doing chores. In that sense, he's trying to manipulate people. While he's just a small boy and it's cute to read about, have you ever found yourself doing the same thing sometimes? What was the result?

2. Liz doesn't think Ian cares enough for Charlie. In a way, she sees only one side of a story, and is accusatory because of it. How does she change throughout the book?

3. After Liz is pulled from her sinking car, and after she's dried off, she realizes that she needs dry clothes and a shower. She offers a simple prayer to God, stating that He knows her basic needs. Do you take your basic needs to God? Do you have a laundry list of wants? Or do you think you should wait until there is something important? What should prayer be?

4. We are to have faith like a child. How do you perceive that? Who in the story had that type of faith? Who did not?

5. What is your first impression of Ian? Does he sound like someone who can and will get the job done? How is that a good thing? How is that a bad thing?

6. In the book of Exodus, Moses' father-in-law, Jethro, tells him to get help, that he's doing too much. George says something similar to Ian, but how does he respond? How should he respond?

7. Ian believes he's better than he was before. Do you agree? Why?

8. Liz is afraid that she'll fail Charlie. Do you see her doing that? What do you think she should be doing or thinking?

9. Liz learns that she can do all things with God's help. Read Philippians 5:12-14 and ask yourself how the verses affect you. What can you attempt today with God's help?

10. Charlie makes a deal with God that he'll tell what happened to his father and God will protect him. Charlie is just an innocent boy, but what was your reaction when you read that? Have you ever made a deal with God? Is it the right thing to do?

11. Liz admits she was wrong when she is found on the trail. She even goes as far as to thank Ian for pointing out the fault. Have you ever done that? What was the result?

12. Liz needs confidence, but she doesn't realize how courageous she is when she thanks Ian for pointing out her fault. What is Ian's reaction? What would you do in his place?

13. When Ian brings Charlie down to Moss Point, he alters the boy's appearance. The results are mixed, though. Now the killer has several boys to choose from, and Liz is scared he'll kill them all. What Bible stories does this remind you of? What did God do in those situations? How were those two stories connected? How were Moses and Jesus connected?

14. What stopped the random killings in this story?

15. Do you think Liz was right to go after Charlie even though the authorities told her not to? Why or why not?

LARGER-PRINT BOOKS!

GET 2 FREE
LARGER-PRINT NOVELS
PLUS 2 FREE
MYSTERY GIFTS

Love Inspired®
SUSPENSE
RIVETING INSPIRATIONAL ROMANCE

Larger-print novels are now available...